"Oh, no, you don't!"

"Yes, yes, yes!"

"Aaii! Little devil!"

"Big bully! Eeep! Noooo..."

Breathless with laughter, Nick and Cami wrestled across the wide bed in a tangle of legs and bedclothes and seeking fingers. Inevitably Nick's superior weight and strength triumphed, and he pinned his panting wife firmly on her back beneath him.

His whispered "Give up?" was a mere formality.

"I surrender," she murmured, but the gleam in her eyes was triumphant...

Lee Damon *describes herself as "a slightly eccentric New England Yankee with an overdeveloped sense of humor, a post-grad degree in chutzpa, and a total lack of interest in domesticity." What does she do all day? "When I'm not hanging out in bookshops or arguing with my twenty-one-year-old son, I read, write, and try to dream up sensuous scenes, riveting repartee, and witty one-liners."*

Dear Reader:

What better month than February, the most romantic time of year, to celebrate a TO HAVE AND TO HOLD mini-anniversary! We started publishing TO HAVE AND TO HOLD only five months ago, and already it's become a highly acclaimed romance line.

Your letters are providing some interesting insights into its success. Many of you were looking forward to TO HAVE AND TO HOLD because of its unique concept of married love, and we're delighted to hear that the books meet your expectations. Others of you wondered if stories of marriage would be as exciting and romantic as those of courtship, and we're equally pleased to hear that TO HAVE AND TO HOLD has convinced you they can be!

In both TO HAVE AND TO HOLD and SECOND CHANCE AT LOVE we strive to bring you the best in romantic fiction. It's our aim to make all our books of such consistently high quality that you'll be as eager to try our exciting new writers as you will be to follow your tried-and-true favorites.

We also work at giving you variety—the spice of life! Within each line we offer a range of approaches—from romances that will tug your heartstrings to those that will tickle your funny bone, from love stories that will set your pulse racing to those that will wrap you in gentle splendors . . .

When you finish our books each month, we hope you feel totally satisfied, as if you've just experienced the best of the many wonderful things love has to offer. So why not take a few minutes to jot down your thoughts about our books and authors and send them along to us. Your opinions are what guide us.

To all our readers, we wish you a most romantic Valentine's Day.

Warmest regards,

Ellen Edwards

Ellen Edwards
TO HAVE AND TO HOLD
The Berkley Publishing Group
200 Madison Avenue
New York, N.Y. 10016

LADY
LAUGHING EYES
LEE
DAMON

**SECOND CHANCE AT LOVE
BOOK**

Second Chance at Love books by
Lee Damon

LAUGH WITH ME, LOVE WITH ME   #120

LADY LAUGHING EYES

First edition published February 1984

First printing

"Second Chance at Love," the butterfly emblem, and "To Have and to Hold" are trademarks belonging to Jove Publications, Inc.

Printed in the United States of America

To Have and to Hold books are published by
The Berkley Publishing Group
200 Madison Avenue, New York, NY 10016

This one's for Melissa, my No. 1 Fan-under-Twenty, who is lovely, lissome proof that Maine girls are every bit as awesome as those famous California girls!

MY THANKS TO:

Priscilla Clark—Melissa's somewhat stunned mother and my friend, mentor, and voice of practicality—for her research assistance and for her hospitality and tour-guiding while I renewed my acquaintance with Portland and its environs.

Craig Milos and Ralph Clarke of Keepers II in Marlborough, Massachusetts, for letting me borrow ideas from their intriguing menu.

MY APOLOGIES, DEAR READERS, BUT . . .

The Old Port Exchange is a very real and fascinating section of Portland, Maine, and its architecture and ambience are much as I've described them herein. It's a delightful place for lunch and an afternoon of browsing if you're ever in Portland. However, please don't use up your time looking for Harborside Lane or the shops and restaurants named in this book; interesting though they may sound, I'm afraid I made them all up.

In an early book of mine, I named and described a hauntingly lovely piece of music, and eventually I received a wonderful fan letter from a seventy-year-old lady who had expended some time and effort to find a recording of that music—which had been a figment of my ever-fertile imagination. Now, before anyone else goes rushing out to the record stores in a futile search, please be advised that the marvelous musical group mentioned in the latter part of this book is another of those fertile figments!

Once Upon a Hot July...

"THANK YOU. DO come in again when you're in the area."

Cami let her friendly smile fade as the coolly elegant woman left the shop, letting the screen door snap shut behind her. Watching her step off the covered porch into the full heat of the July sun, Cami wondered how the woman contrived to look so well groomed and dry in the ninety-degree temperature and high humidity.

"Enough is enough," she muttered, swinging around and stomping resolutely toward the small office at the rear of the shop. She pushed the door almost closed and hitched up the long, full skirt of her colonial-style cotton dress. The wide waistband of the double petticoats was damp with perspiration, and she had to struggle for a minute to release the fasteners. Finally, with a sigh of relief, she let the offending articles slide to the floor and stepped out of them.

"Authenticity is one thing," she said to the big tiger

1

cat sprawled comfortably across the desk, "but smothering to death is something else."

She shook out the petticoats and draped them over a hook on the wall, then looked at herself in the full-length mirror on the back of the door. Not bad, as long as I stand up straight, she thought, checking the length of the gown. Without the fullness of the underskirts, the hem just touched the floor. At least it had short sleeves, and the low, rounded neckline was reasonably cool. Now that she'd shed the petticoats and had on only a thin bra and bikini panties under the dress, she decided that it just might be bearable.

Her long, dark brown hair was piled up in a bun on the top of her head, and she tucked a few stray, damp wisps back into the pins. She wrinkled her nose at her reflection and laughed out loud. Not even the upswept hair and the long dress could make her look taller than five feet two. She knew that her lack of inches, coupled with her slim figure and wide hazel eyes, gave the impression that she was years younger than her actual age of twenty-two.

She scowled and shook her head at her reflection. "Vanity, nothing but vanity," she scolded her image. "Count your blessings, Cami Anders, and stop fussing about the things you can't help. So you're not beautiful, or even pretty, and you hate being called cute. So what? You're healthy and young, and you'll never have to worry about where your next meal is coming from. You've got a brand new college degree and a whole world to explore, once you decide which way to go first. Pea-brain! So what if you look like an overgrown elf; there's bound to be a man somewhere who's got a thing for elves. In the meantime . . ."

Cami whirled around, scooping up the cat and swinging him around in a tight waltz turn. He blinked at her reproachfully as she laughed and said happily, "In the meantime, Tigger, I've got one more summer to help Aunt Sarah and Uncle Phil with the shop and to roam around the Berkshires, and then in the fall... well, who knows? Maybe I'll take a trip to California and look up some old friends and see if there's an interesting job around for a history major. On the other hand, what do you think about Europe? This is the time to go there, before I get tied down in a real job. I could wander around and see all the things I've read about. Bet fall's nice over there; not too many tourists, no crowds in the museums. Maybe I could rent a car and explore some offbeat places. What do you think, cat? Sound like a good idea?"

She laughed again as the big cat yawned in her face and squirmed to get down. Dropping him back onto the desk, she rolled him over and rubbed his belly. Her eyes blurred momentarily with remembered grief as she thought of her parents, whose careful planning had made it possible for her to consider spending several months in Europe. They had been archaeologists and had died in an earthquake while on a dig in Chile when Cami was seventeen. They had left her with happy, loving memories and a comfortable trust fund that would provide her with a modest income for the rest of her life. Her favorite aunt and uncle—her father's brother, Philip Anders, and his wife, Sarah—had been named as her guardians and had brought her back east to live with them in their lovely old home in the Berkshire Hills of western Massachusetts.

Hearing the distinctive snap of the screen door, Cami turned to leave the office. Her lingering memories of the past five years brought a smile to her face as she stepped forward to greet her customer. They had been good years—full of the loving interest and guidance of her aunt and uncle, the fun of making new friends and exploring a countryside very different from her native California, and the busyness of her years at college. She'd enjoyed helping out in the Anders' antique shop in West Stockbridge, a restored Yankee Market Village that had become a major tourist attraction in the Berkshire Hills area.

The only problem, she thought, was the hot costume she had to wear in the middle of a July heat wave. She pushed the high-speed button on the oscillating fan as she walked past it, wishing for the four-thousandth time for air conditioning.

By two o'clock the mercury in the porch thermometer was inching past the ninety-six mark, and Cami was seriously considering closing up for the rest of the day. She felt as if she were melting. For the fourth time she went into the small lavatory to run cold water over her wrists and wipe off her face and neck with a moistened cloth. Returning to the shop, she backed up to the fan and lifted her skirt, letting the moving air cool her damp legs. She closed her eyes and concentrated on a vision of a babbling brook tumbling into a deep, dark forest pool and—

The sound of the screen door brought her eyes open, and she looked up into the amused gray eyes of that being so beloved of fortune-tellers: a tall, dark, and handsome stranger. It was so much the re-creation of half the plots in the Regencies she read—the hoydenish young heroine surprised in an embarrassing situation by the oh-so-suave hero—that Cami began to laugh. Caught up in her vision and encouraged by his smile, she let her dress fall back into place and stepped forward, holding one hand out, palm down, and sweeping her skirt to the side with the other hand as she dipped in a graceful curtsy.

"Welcome to our humble shop, my lord," she said demurely, unable to keep her laughter from dancing in her eyes. In her mental image, his tall, broad-shouldered, lean-hipped figure was clad in polished riding boots, buckskin breeches, a close-fitting coat, and a starched white cravat, rather than in pale blue tailored slacks and a white polo shirt. She could almost see a curly-brimmed beaver hat resting on the thick waves of his dark hair.

For the first time in the twenty-eight years of his carefully planned, rigorously controlled life, Nick de Conti forgot who he was and reacted instinctively. Enchanted with this adorable creature who seemed to have stepped out of another century, he moved forward to take her hand, bowing over it as he raised her from her curtsy.

"It is entirely my pleasure, my lady," he murmured, turning her hand as he brought it to his mouth and pressing a lingering kiss in her palm. Still holding her hand, he straightened up, looked down at her delighted smile, and was lost. With a vague idea of playing for time to regain his equilibrium, he continued the game.

"My lady . . . what?" he wondered aloud, looking her over carefully with a teasing grin. "As I recall, gentlemen often gave a lady a special name to denote an outstanding characteristic. Sooo . . . in another time, you might have been . . . let's see . . . Lady Honey Pot? No. I have a feeling you're not always sweet, not with that firm little chin. Now, now, stop laughing," he chided. "This is serious business. We have to decide on just the right name for you. Lady Sunshine for that smile that lights up your face? Ah, but then there's all that dark hair piled atop your head. Lady Sunshine must have blond hair."

"Lady Shrimp?" suggested Cami, gazing up at him and trying unsuccessfully to keep a straight face. "Lady Half-Pint?"

"How mundane. No, if we were going to roman-

ticize your size, it would have to be...Lady Petite
Venus, I think."

He caught her other hand and held her arms wide,
leaning back to sweep her from head to toe with an
assessing look. "Yes, that's a possibility," he said
thoughtfully. "At least, as near as I can tell through
all that skirt. Slim, but with lovely, graceful curves,
not too much, not too little...Are you blushing, my
lady?"

"You're too much!" Cami gasped, laughing again.

Nick became very still, his gray eyes dark and
intent on her face. Slowly he brought her hands together, holding them easily in one of his, and gently
drew her closer. He cupped her chin in his free hand
and tipped her face up as he bent his head.

"I know the name now," he said softly, pausing in
his downward movement. "It's the first thing I saw,
and it epitomizes you: Lady Laughing Eyes. It's perfect."

His warm mouth touched hers in a breath of a kiss;
then he lifted his head just enough to meet her be-
mused gaze. *"My* Lady Laughing Eyes," he claimed
huskily before his mouth possessed hers in a deep
communion that was both a conquest and a surrender.

By the time he drew back and let her feet touch
the floor again, Cami felt fuzzy-headed and wobbly-
kneed and found herself clinging to his shoulders as
the only stable element in her surroundings. It wasn't
that she'd never been kissed before. She had, many
times, but not even Andy Larsen, with whom she'd
believed herself in love during much of her junior year
in college, had ever made her feel like this. Although
she and Andy had never reached the point of total
intimacy, they had come close a few times, but never,
even at his most passionate, had he made the blood
sing in her veins or her insides melt in a searing heat.

Cami's lashes fluttered wildly as she blinked the haze from her vision and stared up into hot charcoal eyes, their blatant desire touched with wonder and disbelief. With a startled "Oh!" she realized that she was still pressed against the full length of his muscular body, and that the look in his eyes wasn't the only evidence of his passion.

She felt his muscles flex under her hands as his arms tightened around her, and she had a fleeting thought that maybe she should push him away. After all, she'd never seen him before in her life. She didn't even know his name. On the other hand...

Before she gathered her scattered wits enough to make a decision, the ringing telephone settled the matter for her. They both froze, and then Cami unclenched her hands from his shoulders and began to ease away from him. Reluctantly he let his arms slide from around her and stepped back.

Cami forced her recalcitrant feet to move toward the office. She only half heard the brief message from her aunt's friend. Most of her attention was fixed on the reflection in the mirror of her flushed cheeks and dazzled eyes. Absently she said good-bye and hung up the phone, wondering if she'd imagined the man and that passionate kiss. Things like that simply didn't happen in the middle of an ordinary day to a merely "cute" young woman. They happened to beautiful, elegantly tall women in romantic candlelight with the sound of violins in the background.

"It's the heat," she told the dozing Tigger. "I'm hallucinating. I'll walk out there and find the shop empty. Won't I?"

Tigger offered no reassurance beyond a lazy blink of his yellow eyes. With a fatalistic shrug, she stepped through the doorway... and saw the figment of her imagination waiting for her.

Across fifteen feet of cluttered floor space Cami stared at him with a mixture of curiosity, amazement, and an odd feeling of discovery. Her perceptions seemed suddenly sharpened. Part of her was hesitant; part of her was filled with eagerness, as if she were on the brink of a great new adventure.

She saw things that she hadn't noticed at first: the extreme depth of his tan, which indicated a naturally swarthy skin and emphasized his gray eyes with devastating impact; the unusual size of his hands, with their long, supple fingers giving an impression of strength and agility; and, most of all, the aura of powerful virility, tightly leashed and controlled but with a strong hint that it could break loose at any moment in a blaze of wild emotion.

Cami closed her fists on handfuls of her skirt as she felt a jolt of fearful excitement. She had never met a man even remotely like this one, and she had no idea what to do next, how to handle him—if he could be handled at all—or how to handle herself. She desperately wanted to be back in his arms to see if the first time had been a fluke, but simultaneously she wanted to dash for the back door and escape before it was too late. Before she had time to get bogged down in figuring out too late for what and which way to run, he started walking toward her, weaving his way through the array of antiques and artifacts separating them.

"I'm Nick de Conti. I'm twenty-eight, in excellent condition, have all my own teeth and hair, and I've been looking for you for years, Lady Laughing Eyes. All over the world—in London and Paris and Rome, Vienna, St. Petersburg, Bombay, Tokyo and Sydney, and all the major cities in North and South America. Who would ever have thought I'd finally find you in an antique shop in the Berkshires!"

He pulled a stunned Cami into his arms and nuzzled

the sensitive hollow beneath her ear, whispering, "Let's get out of here, *cara mia*. It's been too long, but even so, I can't make love to you for the first time in the middle of a shop."

"You . . . I . . . Wait! . . . You can't . . . I'm not . . ."

The sheer outrageousness of his intentions snapped Cami out of the romantic daze she'd been in since the first moment she'd laid eyes on him. Struggling determinedly, she finally managed to break away from his binding arms and step back, panting and pushing distractedly at her tumbling hair. When he moved toward her with arms outstretched and an indulgent smile, Cami grabbed the first thing that came to hand and waved it at him threateningly.

"You stay right there! You're totally unhinged, you know! A certifiable bedlamite if ever I saw one!"

"What do you intend to do with that?" he asked, eyeing with interest the long-handled carved wooden dipper that was coming perilously close to banging him on the nose.

He noted the angry sparks flashing in his darling's lovely eyes and decided that perhaps he had been just the tiniest bit precipitate. A temporary retreat was called for until he could make his ultimate intentions clear. But not too much of a retreat, he thought, as he moved a couple of steps to the side and sat on the edge of an oak rolltop desk, folding his arms across his chest and waiting patiently for his lady to calm down.

"Aren't you going to tell me your name?" he asked. "Not that I object to calling you Lady Laughing Eyes, but I don't think they'll accept it on the application for a marriage license."

His lips twitched with the effort of holding back a smile. There was no question about it, he mused; she was adorable even open-mouthed and boggle-eyed. He was delighted with the signs of a lively personality and a rather volatile temperament. At the very least he would never be bored—even out of bed. In bed he wasn't worried about. He'd sensed the passion in her, unawakened as yet, but definitely there in the simmering eyes and that delectable mouth. He'd felt it stirring and rising as he'd held her in his arms and kissed her for the first time. She was the one. He knew it. Everything in him called out to her. All he had to do was convince her of the inevitability of *them*, and then they could get on with making their own magic.

Cami's mind finally snapped into gear, and she closed her mouth with an audible click. Clutching the dipper even tighter, she watched him warily. Not for a moment did she believe he was serious. It was just a new approach, and she would let him know that she wasn't taken in by it for a second.

"You've been in the sun too long, Mr. de Conti. Why don't you just relax for a few minutes, and I'm sure you'll feel much better." She struggled to keep her voice calm and soothing. "You shouldn't say things like that, you know. Someone might misunderstand and—"

"How can you misunderstand a proposal of marriage? I thought it was very clear. Perhaps it wasn't romantic enough?" His eyes gleamed with deviltry. "Should I do it properly and go down on one knee?"

"Don't you dare!" yelled Cami, losing her cool completely as he started to drop to his knee. "You can't possibly be serious! You don't even know me! I never saw you in my life until you walked in that door. You can't propose to a total stranger. It's—"

"It's a bit unusual, perhaps, in the normal course of things, but there's nothing normal about us. I told you, *cara*, I've been looking for you for—"

"Balderdash! How could you be looking for me

when you don't even know my name?"

"So what is it?"

"Cami...Cami Anders...Camille. My mother was bitten by Greta Garbo. You're quite totally queer in your attic, you know. Do your people know where you are? Should I call someone to come and get you?"

Nick's burst of laughter distracted Cami just long enough for him to lean forward quickly, catching her unaware as he whisked the dipper away with one hand and secured a firm hold around her waist with his other arm. Despite the hands she braced against his chest, he gently drew her closer to him.

"Shhh, my little lady, not so much yelling and temper. I wouldn't dream of hurting you in any way. On the contrary, I want nothing more than to cherish you and to teach you to love me." He stroked her hair back, tipping her face up so he could brush a kiss across her mouth. "Oh, sweet Cami, we are going to have such a marvelous life together."

*. . . and their golden summer ended
with the first chill of autumn.*

Cami sat cross-legged in the middle of the big bed and watched Nick sleep. She was perfectly happy watching Nick do anything: sleep, walk, talk, laugh, scowl, yell, run, swim, play the piano, and especially make love to her. She was, she readily admitted, totally besotted with the man. Oh, yes. Why else would she have let him sweep her off her feet with all the romantic élan of the most dashing of Regency rakes and charm her into marrying him sixteen days after they met?

She still didn't quite believe it all, despite the fact

that yesterday had been their eighth-week anniversary. Within days of their first meeting she had known that life with Nick would be like riding a perpetual loop-the-loop. *Volatile,* she thought, was the one word she could use to describe him. Exuberantly boyish one minute, intensely sensual the next, and two minutes later he'd forgotten the world existed while he ana-lyzed music in his mind. And no sooner had she begun to get a handle on him, when—wham!—she discov-ered just who Nick de Conti really was.

Cami smiled ruefully to herself as she remembered her chagrin on the day Nick took her to the rehearsal at Tanglewood. She knew very little about classical music and the international concert circuit, but some-how, some way, something should have alerted her when she saw the gleam in Nick's eyes as he an-swered, "Play the piano" to her question about what he did for a living. When he invited her to the rehearsal at the Berkshire Music Center, the summer home of the Boston Symphony Orchestra, she had blithely as-sumed that he played piano with the orchestra—which, in fact, he did . . . as the guest soloist for a pair of week-end concerts.

Even with her limited knowledge of the art she could sense his mastery of both the piano and the music. But it wasn't until she attended the post-concert party and listened to the accolades of the critics and symphony aficionados that she began to see that Nick was considered one of the superstars of the interna-tional concert stage. Then, as the evening wore on, she realized something else. These were people of great wealth, position, and influence—and Nick was talking with them, reminiscing, joking, and compar-ing travel experiences as if he'd known them all his life. She discovered on their way home that he had.

The pale glow of dawn through the east windows

was brightening the room, and Nick turned farther onto his side, burying his face in the pillow. Cami reached out to tug the blanket up over his bare shoulder, and then snuggled deeper into his cashmere robe, which she had wrapped around her nakedness to ward off the early chill on this late September morning. She turned her head to look out through the sliding glass doors that led onto the second-floor deck. In the steadily increasing light she could see the full sweep of the long, sloping field that led down to the river, and the brilliant fall colors of the bordering trees.

I wish we could stay here. The thought had been flitting in and out of her mind for the past few days, ever since Nick had told her that he'd be taking her home to his family estate on the Connecticut shore on Sunday. His family had returned three days ago after spending the summer on the Italian Riviera. Cami wondered for the umpteenth time what they had thought when Nick called them with the news of his marriage. To all her questioning he only answered, "They were surprised, or perhaps I should say stunned. Don't worry, *cara.* How can they help but love you?"

She stifled a groan of frustration when she remembered his laughing unconcern as she tried to point out to him that his family might not be as delighted as he hoped. After all, she was a far cry from the type of woman they probably expected him to choose for a wife.

"I've never been within a mile of the kind of society you grew up in," she'd argued. "I wouldn't know what to do with the sort of money you're used to, or how to live the way you do. I don't even know beans about your music!"

"You'll learn," he'd replied absently, his attention fixed on finding the hidden catch to her chain belt. The discussion ended thirty seconds later as the belt, together with her silk jumpsuit, hit the floor and she hit the couch on her back with a laughing, aroused Nick on top of her.

He'd been equally adept at avoiding any serious discussion of her doubts and anxieties since then. Alternately teasing her and loving her, he'd fended off all her questions with a blithe "Stop fretting so, my Lady Laughing Eyes. Just be yourself, and you'll enchant them all. Right now I want to enjoy our last few days of total privacy. Come on, *carissima*, let's make love in the meadow!"

Her eyebrows drew together in a slight frown as she recalled those words. The exuberant romp in the sunlit meadow had driven his comment from her mind until just now, and she wondered what he had meant by the remark about privacy. It sounded as if they wouldn't have any in Connecticut, but that couldn't be right. One of the few questions he'd answered had been her inquiry as to where they'd live. She knew that the estate included what Nick called "the main house" and several smaller houses. She and Nick would have quarters in the main house, which was also occupied by his parents and his youngest sister. His two married brothers and their families had their own homes on the estate, as did his married sister and her husband and children. Some of the people who worked for the de Contis lived in the other houses.

Unless the place was really huge, thought Cami, it probably would be difficult to find much privacy with all those people around. She wondered what "separate quarters" meant. An apartment? A wing to themselves? Why couldn't they have a house of their own like the other married couples? Why did Nick want to stay in the main house? Maybe he thought it would be easier, since they'd be away on his concert tours so often.

Cami sighed wistfully as she looked again at the

peaceful scene beyond the deck. The first rays of the rising sun flamed the trees into blazing color, and she wished once more that they could stay here in this comfortable, isolated country house, just the two of them, where they could do what they wanted when they wanted.

Her melancholy train of thought was interrupted as Nick stirred and turned onto his back, his eyes blinking open in the bright sunlight flooding into the room. Cami smiled into his sleepy, rainwater-gray eyes. It was a positive crime for those eyelashes to be wasted on a man.

"Hi," she said softly. "I was beginning to wonder if you'd ever wake up."

He yawned and stretched, sending the bedclothes sliding down to his waist, baring his bronzed chest with its thick furring of dark curls. As Cami reached out to trail teasing fingers down the narrowing path of hair over his stomach, the robe she was wearing parted, and Nick came fully awake as he took in her provocative position and her state of undress.

"Surely, my sexy elf, you could have thought of some interesting way of waking me," Nick teased, stroking questing fingers up the inside of her thigh. "After all the attention I've devoted to broadening your education..."

He paused to grin at Cami's gasping "Nick!" as his agile fingers found their target.

"...widening your horizons..."

His voice trailed off into a deep chuckle as she wriggled helplessly, half moaning, half laughing under his expert onslaught.

"...and expanding your—"

His teasing ended in a grunt as Cami tumbled onto his chest, her fingers sliding over his ribs in search of his ticklish spots.

"Oh, no, you don't!"

"Yes, yes, yes!"

"Aaii! Little devil!"

"Big bully! Eeep! Noooo . . ."

Breathless with laughter, they wrestled across the wide bed in a tangle of legs and bedclothes and seeking fingers. Inevitably Nick's superior weight and strength triumphed, and he pinned his panting wife firmly on her back underneath his fully aroused body. He looked down into her glowing face, half hidden under the tumbled mass of her long hair, and caught his breath at the heated shimmer of her hazel eyes.

His whispered "Give up?" was a mere formality; he was already releasing her wrists, lifting some of his weight from her chest, brushing her hair away from her face. He touched his mouth lightly against hers, flicking the tip of his tongue teasingly across her lips.

"I surrender," she murmured, but the gleam in her eyes was triumphant as she pulled her knees back farther to cradle his passionate hardness more intimately against her.

With a groan Nick took her mouth in a deep, exploring kiss, and, at the touch of her urgent hands on his buttocks, he joined their bodies with a slow, powerful thrust of his hips, moving strongly within her, pacing their climb to her answering beat, finally sliding his hands under her bottom to urge her to a wild tempo that took them over the peak.

Long moments later, after their breathing had slowed and Nick had shifted to lie beside her, Cami again felt the chill of the room, even cooler now against her sweat-dampened skin. Shivering, she scrambled to free the blanket from the tangled bedclothes and pull it over them as she dived into Nick's welcoming arms.

"Quick!" she gasped against his neck. "Warm me up, please."

"I thought I just did," he said with a deep chuckle. "However," he murmured as he slowly ran his large, warm hands over her, "I'm willing to give it another go. Is this...hmmm, now there's an interesting spot...any better or...and another one...Oh, poor thing, it's really cold...Ah, maybe I should kiss it and..."

His commentary shifted into the soft Italian cadence he used only during lovemaking, and Cami felt herself blushing as she recognized some of the words and phrases he'd laughingly translated for her one night.

"Is that any way to talk to your wife?" she chided, burying her hands in his thick hair and tugging on it gently.

"Mmmm. You wouldn't want me to say these things to someone else's wife, would you?" he growled against her breast.

"No-oohh, ohh, yesss...do that...just like that..."

The last thing Cami felt right now was cold. Nick's warm, wet tongue playing around her nipple was sending fiery frissons racing over her skin. She twisted and arched her back, still holding his head against her breast, and felt his hands lifting and moving her until she could feel the tickle of his chest hair against her stomach. He locked his arms around her and rolled onto his back, coming to rest with his face buried between her breasts.

"Eeee! Nick...you're all bristly...Aahhh, what are you doing?"

"Getting you where I want you."

His guiding hands were urging her upright and shifting her backward on her knees until she was straddling his hips. Cami let go of his hair and trailed her hands down across the smooth skin of his neck and shoulders until she could twine her fingers in the thick mat of curls on his chest. She kept her eyes on his,

watching the gray deepen to charcoal. His voice was
hoarse as he gasped a plea in Italian, but before she
could translate it his hands were on her hips, lifting
her and slowly guiding her down onto him. She forgot
what little Italian she knew, as well as most of her
English, as she felt him filling her, and she began to
move her hips in tiny circles within his enclosing
hands.

"Cara, this is no time to tease," he groaned as she
resisted his urgent hands and barely moved on him.

"Shhh, Mr. Impatient. You put me up here, so now
we'll do it my way."

Holding on to the last shreds of her control, Cami
leaned forward to swing her long hair back and forth
across his bare stomach. A gasping laugh escaped her
as his muscles rippled, and then her control fled as
he arched against her and his hands closed tightly
around her hips, moving her into a crescendoing coun-
terpoint to his strong rhythm until they soared together
into a vibrating finale.

Cami collapsed into a boneless heap on Nick's
heaving chest, her hair spreading out to cloak his
shoulders. After a few moments he began a calming
stroking of her back, settling her more comfortably
on top of his long body. He brought one hand up to
brush her hair away from her face, and he felt the
wetness on her cheek.

"Are you crying, love?" he whispered, tilting her
head up so he could look into her eyes. "What's wrong?
Did I hurt you, Cami?"

"No, no, you didn't... It was beautiful... truly,
Nick... I just... just..."

She hid her face against his neck, sniffing and
blinking back the rest of her tears, feeling like a perfect
idiot. She wasn't even sure why she was crying, but
all of a sudden —

"Please, my darling, can't you tell me what's wrong?" Nick coaxed, wrapping his arms around her securely.

"I'm not sure. All of a sudden I was afraid. I'm so happy here with you, and it's been so beautiful and full of laughter and love and doing just what we want and—Oh, Nick, it won't be like this after tomorrow, and I suddenly felt that it was all going to change, and I had to hold on to every minute and every hour and—"

"Shhh, now, sweetheart," Nick murmured soothingly. "My own feisty elf, it's all going to be fine. You're nervous about meeting my family, but they'll love you just as much as I do. Well, almost as much, anyway. Remember, Cami, they're your family now, too. My brothers will tease you, and my sisters will take you shopping and gossip with you. You'll enjoy that, won't you?"

"Oh, Nick. I'll . . . I'll try, although shopping and gossip aren't exactly my favorite pastimes. What else do they like to do? You've told me so little about your family, and here I am meeting them tomorrow."

"Well, Marguerita of course has her family, and . . . and they do whatever women do," he said vaguely. "I think they work on some charity committees and things with Mother." His voice grew more positive. "My mother, now, you'll love. She's a wonderful woman. So understanding, so supportive, so wise about everything. I told you, didn't I, how carefully she watched over my development when I was very young? That's so important; it's easy to push a child with great talent too hard too soon and ruin his gifts. But she made sure that didn't happen with me, and when it was time for me to start playing concerts, she arranged for Arthur Rossman to manage my career. A good manager is essential. Many fine performers have had their careers and often their talents damaged by poor management."

"And your father? Will he get better?"

"Anything is possible, of course, but the second stroke did considerable damage. The doctors don't think he'll be able to manage again without the wheelchair. However, his mind is still sharp, and he communicates quite well. He'll enjoy your weird sense of humor, *cara,* especially if you do your colonial-belle act. He's always been fascinated with history."

"Then we should get along fine," said Cami in obvious relief. "But amusing your father and shopping and stuff won't take up all that much of my time. I hope I can find something interesting to do—maybe work in an antique shop part-time or—"

"That's out of the question. You must know that, Cami," he chided, tipping her face up and smiling at her indulgently. "The de Conti women do not go out and work. Besides, you'll have enough to keep you busy being my wife, my lover, my own Lady Laughing Eyes, and before too long you'll probably have a baby to amuse you. You'll like that, won't you?"

"Well . . . yes, but . . ." Cami moved to sit beside him, frowning slightly as she looked down at his pleased smile. "But I hadn't thought of having a baby quite this soon. We . . . we've known each other such a short time, Nick. I thought we'd wait awhile, maybe a year or two, so that we could have some time just to be by ourselves."

"Silly elf. There's no problem. You'll have a nursemaid, just as the others do. We'll have plenty of time to be together when I'm not practicing or on tour. Don't worry about it, *cara.* You must trust me to know what's right. Mother always said it was best to have the children when you're young, and she's far more experienced in these things than you are."

"But, Nick—"

"Now, now, my love, no arguments. Everything will be fine. We love each other, don't we, and that's all that's important."

Disquieted by his rather high-handed, word-of-the-master attitude, Cami wanted to continue the discussion. But what discussion? He was handing down pronouncements. Didn't she have anything to say about anything?

Before she could think of how to word her protest, Nick sat up and swung his long legs out of the bed. "Now that we've settled all that, what would you like to do today? Come along, lazybones; I need my breakfast after all this early morning exercise." He reached across the bed to swat her lightly on her backside. "Be a good elf and I'll take you skinny-dipping later in the pool. That's one thing we won't be able to do at home."

Summoning up a reasonably happy laugh, Cami scrambled off the bed and ran for the shower. Her thoughts, however, were troubled. Somehow in the last few minutes the bright new shine of her marriage had dimmed a little, and she felt a shiver of trepidation as she wondered about tomorrow and their return to Nick's home and her first meeting with his family.

. . . but finally, alone
and despairing, she fled . . .

Cami glanced nervously at her watch yet again. Where was the taxi? It was supposed to be here at two o'clock. From now on every minute counted, and it was already ten past two. She quickly redirected her gaze through the small panes of the oriel window

and scanned the visible portions of the wide drive that
wound through the beautifully landscaped park between the villa and the main gates. A steady stream
of cars, mostly of the luxury variety, moved up the
drive—but no taxi.

Chilled despite her heavy Fair Isle sweater and the
sunlight pouring through the window, Cami wrapped
her arms around her too-thin body and glanced down
through the window to check the activity around the
front entrance and in the forecourt. She'd chosen this
vantage point carefully. The oriel, set in a deep alcove
of her second-floor sitting room, not only gave the
best view of the drive and front door, but allowed her
to remain out of sight of anyone looking into the sitting
room from the hall. Not that she expected anyone to
come searching for her. She'd made it plain that she
had no desire to take part in today's activities.

If Nick had been here, she—No, she wasn't going
to think about Nick, or about Lucianna, or about her
disaster of a marriage. She was going to concentrate
on the here and now. One thing at a time. First she
had to get away without being stopped. Not that Lucianna would try to stop her; her mother-in-law would
probably give her the cab fare. However, the rest of
the family, particularly her friendly but ineffectual
father-in-law, and the guards would definitely prevent
her from leaving by herself. This afternoon would be
her only chance to get out.

Another check of her watch showed that only two
minutes had passed, but it was two minutes too many.
Damn, where was that cab driver? She'd planned
everything so carefully. This mid-October Thursday
was one of two days during the year that the main
gates were left open. So many cars were moving into
and out of the estate that the guards were unable to
keep track of everyone's identity. The Annual Autumn

House Tour, a fund-raising event sponsored by the
Fairfield County Historical Society, was a three-day
affair that climaxed on the third afternoon at *I Venti
di Mare*. Sea Winds, as it was locally known, was
the de Conti family's walled and guarded forty-five-
acre estate on the Connecticut shore.

Cami noted that there were still a number of people
wandering around the forecourt, admiring the lovely
displays of mums and the brilliant fall foliage of the
trees in the park while they waited their turn on the
guided tours through the principal rooms of the house.
She wondered if any of them would realize how cold
those rooms full of art and antiques could be if you
tried to live in them as an unwelcome outsider. Or
would they see only the surface charm and beauty of
the thirty-room Italian villa that had been built in 1820
by exiled Pietro de Conti to remind him of his home-
land?

From her suite in the west wing, she could neither
hear nor see the activity on the east terrace, where the
caterers were setting up the buffet tea that would be
served at three o'clock. However, she could easily
visualize the scene from years past when she had been
one of the family members greeting the two- to three-
hundred visitors, making them welcome and ensuring
that everyone enjoyed this rare occasion. She remembered the year it rained and they had to move the event
into the ballroom. But on a mild, sunny day like this,
the buffet would be held on the expansive three-level
east terrace with its spectacular view of Long Island
Sound, framed by the dark cedars and white marble
sculptures bordering the plush green lawn of the two-
hundred-foot-wide *grande allée*. At this time of year
the scene was even more dramatic, with the dark green
of the cedars silhouetted against the glowing oranges
and reds of the many maple trees that had been planted

over the years to provide summer shade and autumn beauty.

Painfully vivid and wholly unwelcome, a picture filled her mind of that first October tea four years ago, a few days after Nick had brought her to *I Venti di Mare* to live. That day she had finally and fully understood just what kind of an alien lifestyle she'd stumbled into with her whirlwind marriage to a man she barely knew. She closed her eyes against the memory of Nick, tall and leanly elegant in his hand-tailored tweeds, moving through the throng of obviously wealthy, obviously "society" visitors as he dispensed charm and hospitality in equal measure. And, oh, how she remembered those women in their designer suits, "little" furs, and discreet afternoon jewels—and their not-so-discreet eyes eating Nick up as they flirted and fawned over him. Yes, indeed, and why not? He had it all: wealth, fame, extraordinary talent, masses of charm, and that dark, compelling handsomeness. She remembered how bewildered she'd felt, wondering what she was doing there in the middle of a scene by John O'Hara, looking at all those coolly sophisticated women and wondering even more why Nick had ever married *her*.

Cami violently forced down the memory and opened her eyes. She scanned the drive again and caught a flash of yellow and blue. At last, the taxi was here. At the rate the cars were moving, it would be a couple of minutes before it reached the side entrance. Just time enough, she decided as she turned from the window and ran to the connecting door to her bedroom.

Moving swiftly, she crossed to the bureau and snatched up the silk scarf she'd left ready, tying it Gypsy-style over her dark hair. Her quick glance in the mirror was to make sure that the scarf covered the front and sides of her hair; she carefully avoided looking at her too-large eyes, her pale, thin face, or the pinched, bitter line of her mouth. Shrugging into her gray suede jacket, she flipped the collar up, effectively hiding her long, thick braid. She pulled the two notes out of her hip pocket and propped them against the gold-embossed leather jewel case.

She turned away and then hesitated, glancing back at the envelope addressed to Nick. She could see the bulge made by her ring, and for a moment everything blurred. Determinedly she blinked back the tears. No. She'd cried more than enough, and it was better this way. It was over, and now it was time to go.

Within a couple of minutes she had collected her big Ghurka shoulder bag and the matching carryall, scrambled down the concealed fire escape at the end of the west wing, and darted through the shrubbery to the edge of the drive. Squeezing between two parked cars, she climbed into the waiting taxi and directed the driver onto the loop that would take them back to the main drive.

Cami slumped back with a sigh of relief that she'd managed the toughest part: getting out of the house unseen. If her luck held, she thought as she reached into her bag for the oversized sunglasses, the gate guard would be bored by now and wouldn't even look at her. Even if he did, he'd never recognize the oh-so-properly-chic Mrs. Dominic de Conti decked out in faded jeans and a sweater and half hidden under a scarf and glasses.

The driver swung onto the main drive, and Cami knew the gates were just beyond the next curve. She could feel the trembling in her hands, and she clenched them around the heavy leather strap of her bag. She refused to let her mind stray to regrets or second thoughts. Not again. At least not now. She'd been over it all endlessly. One more bitter thought and she'd go right over the edge. Enough was enough.

She was so intent on keeping a lid on her fragile emotional state that she wasn't aware they'd passed through the gates until she felt the car turn and accelerate, and realized that they were on Shore Drive headed for Stamford. As if compelled, she turned to look back, although she knew that the villa couldn't be seen from the road and that even the enclosing wall was hidden by carefully planned landscaping.

Is it really there? Perhaps I dreamed it all. I feel as if I'm in the middle of a nightmare. Oh, Nick, where are you? I need you. I'm falling apart into millions of pieces, and you're on the other side of the world. Why aren't you here telling me it's all a lie? I loved you so much in spite of all the bad times, and I tried so hard to be what you wanted but . . . it isn't me anymore. I'm somebody else, and I think I'm losing my mind. What's happening to me? What happened to us?

*. . . and she wondered
if he would care . . .*

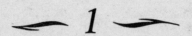

1

"YOU IDIOT FEMALE! How many times have I told you not to climb on chairs? One of these days you're going to break your silly neck!"

Cami froze. The voice, the exasperated words, the long, strong fingers gripping her hips—all were appallingly familiar. Shock was an icy tremor shivering through her body, stopping her breath, and holding her immobile while her numbed mind screamed, *Nick!*

It was only for a few seconds, although it seemed like forever, that Cami balanced on her toes on the sturdy oak kitchen chair, one hand grasping the edge of a shelf while she stretched her other arm over her head to reach for an old glass hurricane lamp on the top shelf. She stared unseeingly at a charming pig stenciled on an antique tin canister, one of several displayed on the ledge directly in front of her. With an almost painful effort, she forced her mind to start functioning again.

Nick? Here? In Portland, Maine? Impossible! This is the last place he'd be. And then from a deep, secretive place in her mind crept the hope that she'd refused to acknowledge for over seven months. *Has he been looking for me? Did he care enough to manage, somehow, to trace me to this unlikely place? And if he did, why's he yelling? Damn. Nothing's changed at all. He's still treating me as if I didn't have a mind of my own.*

The bracing anger surged through her, giving her the strength to lift down the lamp and turn around to face her maddening husband. The air around them fairly crackled with tension, and yet, in some inexplicable way, they seemed at the same time to be cocooned in a great silence. Cami, still held firmly by the hands around her hips, stared down into the face she thought she knew better than her own. Her eyes widened with consternation, and her lips parted on a hard, indrawn breath.

This wasn't the face she remembered! *Her* Nick had never grown a beard or a mustache. On the contrary, her Nick had shaved at least twice a day, often three times if he was performing or if they were late going to bed. And that hair! *Her* Nick had never let his hair grow so long. It was right over the collar of his shirt.

From the little she could see of his face, it looked thinner, the bone structure standing out more prominently from the hollows under the cheekbones and at the temples. Even those long, impossibly curling eyelashes failed to counteract the harsh lines of—could it be bitterness?—that bracketed the straight nose and etched a tracery across the sculpted forehead. The fine lines at the corners of his eyes seemed deeper, and there was an unfamiliar crease between the thick, perfectly curved eyebrows.

With great reluctance, Cami finally let her eyes meet the demanding force of his dark gray gaze. That dark gray said it all. He was furious. One part of her mind concentrated on trying to figure out why he was so obviously enraged. After all, she had only done what he'd wanted her to do, so why all the fire and fury now? The other, self-protective part of her mind rapidly sorted through a collection of opening remarks to find one appropriate for greeting a husband who had rejected her—and had now changed his mind perhaps? Well, the questions would have to wait. Right now...

"Don't be ridiculous, Nick. I've been climbing on chairs for years and haven't broken anything yet," Cami said tartly. "Would you mind? You're going to leave bruises if you don't loosen your hands, and I—"

"Who's going to see them?" he snarled, tightening his grip on her slim hips. "Is that what this has all been about? You've got a new man in your life? No wonder you sneaked off without a word to—"

"I did not *sneak* off!" exploded Cami, her own anger rising to meet his. "I—Oh, no, you don't, Dominic de Conti. You're not going to draw me into one of your convoluted arguments. Just stand back and let me get down. There's a customer waiting for this lamp," she said firmly as the sight of the middle-aged woman waiting at the cash register recalled her to business.

With what sounded suspiciously like a growl, Nick shifted his hands to her waist and swung Cami down from the chair, setting her lightly on her feet in front of him. She looked up at him with a resentful scowl. Despite the beard, some things hadn't changed at all, she thought. He still had that annoying habit of picking her up and putting her down where he wanted her. She still wasn't impressed, and she still wished that she were eight inches taller and forty pounds heavier.

Then let him try to toss her around like a rag doll! He'd probably get a hernia, and it would serve him right!

She tipped her head back and stared up into the stormy eyes almost a foot above her, matching him glare for glare. It was incredible. After all these months he was finally here. She hadn't dared to let herself hope that he'd try to find her, and yet he obviously had. That meant he must care about her at least a little, didn't it? So why was he so mad? For that matter, why was she? Had he hunted her down just to yell at her and manhandle her? Hadn't he learned anything from all this? Oh, hell!

"Cami, I want to—" Nick's demand was cut off by her small, imperiously raised hand.

"You'll have to wait, Nick, until I take care of my customer," she stated, twisting out of his hands and heading purposefully toward the checkout counter.

Cami was barely aware of what she was saying, but she must have made sense, since the customer left a few minutes later with a satisfied smile and a bulging shopping bag. Throughout the transaction, Cami's eyes kept flicking to the far corner of the shop where Nick loitered. She was dismayed at her physical reaction to the sight of his long, lean body, its sinewy musculature enhanced rather than hidden by the tight white jeans and navy and lime golf shirt. Against her will, her unruly mind kept flashing memories of that body, naked, tanned, and heavily matted with curling dark hair. *Behave, dammit. We've got a long way to go before we're back on an intimate basis.* Another quick look at him, taking in the thick furring on his bare forearms, only served to reinforce her memories and tighten her abdominal muscles.

By the time the door closed behind her customer, Cami was working up a fine rage against her wayward senses. She'd been so sure that after these months of peaceful recuperation she'd finally come to terms with her feelings for Nick, that she was at last sensible enough to put those four years she'd spent on an emotional seesaw into perspective, and that she had now developed enough self-awareness to control a purely physical reaction to a good-looking, charismatic male.

Dammit! I'm not going to let him do this to me again! I don't care how sexy-looking he is or how great we were in bed; he was still totally impossible as a husband. Domineering, mule-headed, overbearing, and deaf, dumb, and blind to anything that might upset his carefully tailored lifestyle. Just remember, Camille Anders, that he can turn off all that bone-melting Italian charm in the blink of an eye and flip right out into a roaring temper fit. His mother might have thought that his bouts of artistic temperament were magnificent, but she was never on the receiving end. Too bad. If she had been, she might have smacked him a good one when he was young enough for it to help matters, instead of hovering around him with that doting smile and cooing about his marvelous fire and verve and passion. Thanks to her idiocy, I ended up with the ultimate male chauvinist!

She watched Nick coming toward her with that stalking-cat stride, and she could have kicked herself for wishing, momentarily, that she had dressed in something more elegant than a khaki wraparound skirt and a pale blue cotton-knit shell. When he stopped at the other side of the counter and leaned toward her on his braced hands, she also wished that she'd worn her clogs instead of flat-heeled sandals. In an argument with Nick, every extra inch helped

"Well?" he snapped. "Start explaining, Cami."

So much for Italian charm! "Start explaining what,

Nick?" she asked sweetly, keeping a tight rein on her temper. "Maybe you'd like to explain how you found me here, and why you bothered."

"Why I—" He broke off to mutter something in Italian that Cami was sure she'd rather not understand. "If that isn't one of your typically stupid remarks. One would think, no, expect, that you would have outgrown these adolescent ploys by now. As for finding you," he continued, raising his voice to drown out her indignant protest, "it's a wonder I did. You certainly covered your tracks well. It's taken me months and the help of a very expensive detective to trace you. He wasted almost four months in a necessarily discreet search of California; we naturally assumed you'd run back to your old friends. We never thought of looking in Maine until he traced your college roommate."

He took a deep breath, trying to calm down as he became aware of Cami's increasingly wrathful expression. Almost immediately, however, another source of grievance caught his attention, and he exploded again.

"What have you done to your hair? I don't like it. Why did you do such an appalling thing? It was criminal to cut off your beautiful long hair for that . . . that bird's nest! You had—"

"Now you just hold it, Nick de Conti!" Cami caught herself up with a quick, indrawn breath. That had been just a few decibels below a yell, and she was determined to be dignified and in complete control of her temper. *Damn the man. I never even had a temper until I married him.*

"It's a feather cut," she said with commendable calm. "It's cool and easy to care for, and I like it. So does everyone else. It's also appropriate to my age. Really, Nick, I'm a bit beyond running around with my hair hanging down to my waist, don't you hink? So adolescent," she added blandly.

Why are we talking about my hair? I left him because, among other things, he wanted to marry another woman, and now, the first time he sees me, all he can do is complain about my hair!

"It's atrocious," he snarled, glaring balefully at the mass of short curls covering her head and feathering around her face. The rich, deep brown curls were touched with gold and dark red in the bright June sunlight streaming through the big front window.

Why are we arguing over her hair? She ran out on me seven months ago and disappeared without a trace, with no explanation except for that meaningless note, and we're standing here yelling about hair. Lord, she looks so good—even the hair. She's gained back some weight and looks so much healthier with that tan. If she's done all this for another man, I'll break her neck!

Cami took a deep breath and another half-hitch in the leash on her temper. She managed a small, very small, smile and said lightly, "I can't say I care much for your new hairstyle, either, or for that bushy mess on your face!"

By the end of the sentence her smile had disappeared, and she was looking defiantly belligerent. Nick leaned farther over the counter, looming threateningly above her, his eyes almost black with fury, and Cami took a prudent step backward. Not that she was really afraid of him; she knew he wouldn't dream of hitting her. At least she didn't think he would, although...

He did that one time. Remember? Well, yes, in a way he did, but it wasn't really hitting. It was a spanking. But it hurt like hell. He's got those big, hard hands, and he was madder than a wet wasp. He was sorry afterward, though and—And kissed it all better, so you figure he'll never get mad enough to do it again. Right? Dummy! Take a good look at him. That ridiculous beard is absolutely bristling.

Nick's eyes narrowed as he watched her edge away from him, her big hazel eyes fixed on him warily, and her small, stubborn chin lifted with defensive determination. Struggling to get a firm hold on his flaming temper, he scanned his wife's slim, delicately curved body with a hunger that had been building for months. Suddenly none of it seemed important: why she left, his long frustrating search, this stupid argument. All that mattered was that he had found her again and that, as soon as he could get her someplace where they wouldn't be interrupted at any moment, he'd have her in his arms and be able to lose himself at long last in the hot, welcoming depth of her eager body.

Cami saw the slow change in his expression, and with rapidly returning skill she read the flaring lights in his still-dark eyes correctly. Not that his obviously burgeoning desire was any more comforting than his anger. Nick in *any* kind of a passion was a force to be handled like nitroglycerine—*with extreme care and prepared for it to explode in your face at any moment. What's all this in aid of anyhow? He got what he wanted, didn't he? Or did Oriana defect on him, too?*

"Don't panic, Cami," said Nick, his voice finally pitched at its normal, velvety baritone. He straightened up from his menacing posture and stood casually hipshot with his hands tucked in the front pockets of his jeans. "Just what do you suppose I'm going to do to you? Smack you? Much as I might think you deserve it, you know I wouldn't. At least, you should know—"

"You did once," she snapped

"Oh, come on, woman," he said, shrugging disparagingly. "A couple of wallops on your butt, and—"

"Hard wallops, and it was more than a couple."

"You have to admit I had reason."

"What reason?" she demanded, refusing to give an inch.

"You did throw a brass pot at me, or have you forgotten that part?"

"I didn't throw it *at* you; I threw it *past* you."

"Only because you have rotten aim."

"I do not! And besides, you deserved it; you called me a stupid ninny!"

"Because you were being a ninny at the time. Dammit, Cami," he sighed in exasperation, raking long fingers through his hair, "you're still squabbling like a ten-year-old."

"Oh, you—I like that! Who started this? *You* did, coming in here and shouting at me and criticizing my hair and—"

Cami broke off in mid-yell as she caught sight of a movement beyond Nick's shoulder and realized that two women were about to enter the shop. Muttering imprecations under her breath, she swung around and became very busy rearranging a display of nineteenth-century cast-iron muffin pans.

Calm . . . calm . . . I will be calm. I will not let him push me into another one of those shouting matches. I will not let that overbearing, bossy, impossible man pull off his ridiculous chauvinist act. Never again will I let him treat me like a ninnyhammer. I am twenty-seven years old . . . intelligent . . . knowledgeable . . . cool . . . calm . . . dignified.

"Cami?" murmured the soft baritone voice from above her head.

She plucked a long-handled toasting fork from a nearby rack and turned halfway around, glowering up at Nick, who was standing close enough to block her view of the rest of the shop.

"If you don't get away from me," she hissed, "I swear I'll skewer you!"

"Not even ten years old. More like eight," he chided, deftly whipping the fork out of her loose grip and replacing it on the rack. There was a flash of white in the mass of facial hair, and his voice held unmistakable laughter as he said, "Such passion, *cara!* What's the matter . . . don't you have anyone to fight with anymore?"

"Don't be ridiculous! You know I never liked to fight," Cami muttered, trying to edge around him.

"I'm not so sure about that," he mused with a deep chuckle. "You certainly enjoyed the making up part. I often wondered . . ." He laughed outright at her incensed expression and her incoherent sputtering as she tried to find a suitably scathing comment.

Cami knew that her anger was as much with herself as with him. There was a certain amount of truth in what he said. Not about her liking to fight. She didn't. However, it was undeniable that some of their most memorable and fiercest lovemaking had taken place after their worst arguments. But she wasn't about to admit that to him. At least not until she found out why he was really here. In the meantime . . .

"Let me by, Nick. I've got customers."

Unthinkingly she put her hands on his waist to push him aside, and then hastily yanked them away as she felt his taut body under her palms. She took one quick upward look, met his knowing grin, and promptly blushed furiously. She tried to turn her head away, but he caught her chin and tipped her face up, compelling her to meet his laughing gray eyes.

"It's all right, sweet elf," he purred. "I like you to touch me."

"Nick . . ."

"Oh, well, you're probably right. This isn't the time or place, but later—"

"Dammit, Nick—"

"... we'll have all the privacy we need, and then you can—"

"No!"

"... know me again, just as I'll refresh my memories of you. It's been such a—"

"We can't—"

"No, we can't right now, *cara*. You have customers, remember? Why don't you run along and take care of them. I'll look around while I'm waiting."

Cami stared up at him, totally frustrated but at the same time struggling to hold back a bubble of laughter. Oh, he was impossible! Somewhere in the past few minutes, she realized, Nick's attitude had completely changed. Now he was relaxed, amused, teasing, and utterly nonaggressive. And she didn't trust him an inch. Not with that flashing silvery glint in his eye.

Nick grinned down at her, enjoying her swiftly changing expressions, then moved aside with a bow and a flourish of one hand.

"Business first, my lady," he murmured. "Then we'll take care of pleasure."

"Arrogant ape!" she growled as she slipped past him. Unfortunately, she spoiled her attempt at ferocity with an uncontrollable giggle.

Her fervent hope that he hadn't caught her unintentional reaction to his teasing died a quick death when she heard his deep chuckle and his complacent order, "Take your time, firecracker. I've got all afternoon."

When it became obvious after a few minutes that Cami would be involved with her customers for a while, Nick began wandering around the shop. He already knew, from the detective's report, that Cami and her friend Jean Vernon had opened their shop, Grandma's Kitchen, four months ago, but he hadn't really thought much about what that meant. Now he began examining the array of kitchen tools and equipment displayed on shelves, racks, and tray-topped islands, and reading the descriptive cards positioned near many of the items.

It didn't take him long to realize just what he was seeing. From a handwritten, nearly indecipherable seventeenth-century cookbook to a 1946 state-of-the-art Rival can opener, the shop contained a three-hundred-year history of the American kitchen. As he opened the doors of old oak iceboxes and a beautiful Hoosier cabinet and admired the intricate scrolling on a small cast-iron stove, he began to wonder just how Cami and her partner managed to find all these things.

Fascinated, he spent several minutes examining a display of complex mechanical devices that looked remarkably like ancient instruments of torture. However, the descriptive cards informed him that the various metal and wooden combinations of gears, handles, spikes, knives, and pulleys were actually apple parers/corers/slicers, cherry stoners, and raisin seeders. He cast a doubtful eye at an 1895 Enterprise raisin seeder, wondering if anyone would really use such a thing these days. An apple parer or cherry stoner, on the other hand, seemed eminently practical. Flipping price tags, he thought that twenty to forty dollars was a reasonable amount to pay for something both useful and historical.

"Take two, and I'll give you a good deal."

Nick swung around, laughing, at the sound of Cami's guttural accent. "That's an atrocious Groucho. You do a much better Yogi Bear."

"The story of my life," said Cami with a theatrical sigh. "I wanted to be Farrah Fawcett and ended up playing Peter Pan."

They stared at each other, the laughter slowly fading. Nick brought his hands up to grasp her shoulders and draw her closer, but she braced her hands against his chest to hold him off.

"Oh, *cara*, I've missed you so. Why did you leave like that?"

"I told you why. Didn't you get my note?"

"Note! You call that crazy thing an explanation? 'I don't have to be told twice. Since this is your idea, you take care of the details. If you wanted Chateaubriand, why did you settle for Yankee pot roast?' Not one word of that makes any sense at all. What the hell were you talking about?"

"You know perfectly well what I was talking about. I do think, though, that you might have told me yourself instead of having your mother explain things. She wasn't very nice about it, but then, she never liked me much from the first day I walked in the door."

"Nonsense! You've always had an irrational dislike of my mother, even though she's made every effort, right from the beginning, to help you and teach you—"

At the sound of voices and laughter, Nick broke off the increasingly heated argument. Cami's emphatic "Balderdash!" was, however, easily heard over the chatter of the group of women entering the shop.

"This place is about as private as a zoo," Nick muttered disgustedly. "It's impossible to talk here. How soon can you leave? Can't your partner—Jean, isn't it?—manage for the rest of the day by herself?"

Cami had taken a step away from Nick, but now she glanced around the shop and noted that the women were all happily browsing. Looking up at Nick's impatient expression, she bit back a smile. He did so hate to be balked. Well, for once, he was going to have to do things her way.

"I agree, we can't talk here. For one thing, your bad temper—"

"*My* bad temper!"

". . . will scare off my customers. Besides, it looks like a busy afternoon, and we'll have constant interruptions. But I can't leave until six because—"

"Six!"

". . . Jean won't be back until late afternoon. She's out crawling around in an old barn." Cami stifled a laugh at his bewildered look. "Junky old barns are gold mines when it comes to finding our kind of stuff. Jean and I spend half our time rooting around in them. You wouldn't believe what some people save—thank heavens!"

Nick shook his head in disbelief. "I can't believe you left a beautiful place like *I Venti di Mare* to grub around in dirty barns."

"I didn't. I left—" Cami broke off, distracted by the sight of one of the women obviously looking around for someone to help her. "We can't talk about it now. Why don't you go sightseeing or something and meet me back here at six."

"All right," he agreed reluctantly. He was loath to wait any longer for explanations, but he realized that anything else was impossible. "We'll go out to dinner, someplace quiet where we can talk. You've got a lot of explaining to do, Cami."

She gave him a straight look and said evenly, "So have you, Nick."

Without giving him time to say anything further, she turned on her heel and left him.

At five minutes to six, Cami was still dithering about in the shop's bathroom, poking at her hair and checking her lip gloss. Staring at her wide, apprehensive eyes in the mirror, she muffled a groan as she saw also the unwelcome glint of anticipation. She couldn't, simply *could not*, be looking forward to seeing Nick again. Truly, truly, she didn't want to be

alone with him, didn't want to talk with him, didn't
want to answer questions, discuss the past, or explain . . . what? What was there to explain? He knew—
no matter what he said, he knew—exactly why she'd
left. No way was she going to get involved again with
that impossible man. She'd already been folded, bent,
dog-eared, and stapled, and she wasn't about to issue
another invitation to disaster.

"Featherwit!" she muttered, sticking her tongue out
at her reflection. "Totty-headed twiddlepoop," she
added as she turned away to fuss with the already
straight towels on the wicker rack. "Oh, blast, I've
got to stop reading Regencies. I'm beginning to sound
like Lady Camille van de Twit."

She stepped into the dressing alcove, still muttering
to herself, and reached for her shoulder bag.

"Ready, Cami?"

Startled by the unexpected sound of Nick's voice,
she whirled around, banging her elbow on a shelf
edge. She yelped, and quick tears filled her eyes in
reaction to the sharp pain.

"You . . . now look what you made me do! Ooooo,
that smarts," she moaned, jigging from one foot to
the other.

"Hold still," Nick commanded, trying not to laugh.
"Let me see. Come on, Cami, stop bouncing around
and let me rub it."

"It's not funny, you monster. I probably cracked
it or chipped it, and all you can do is giggle!"

"I've never giggled in my life," he choked, biting
his lip. He finally got a firm grip on her upper arm
and held her still while he massaged her abused elbow.
"Stop glaring at me, *cara,* and don't pull away. You
just hit your crazy bone. It'll feel better in a minute."

"Will you let go of me!" she demanded. Her mind
was already in confusion from surprise and pain, and

now the feeling of Nick's warm, supple hands on her arm was only compounding her problems. She found it more than difficult enough to cope with his presence without having him touch her.

Nick automatically resisted her efforts to pull loose, wrapping his long fingers more securely around her arm. Something, perhaps a hint of desperation in her struggles, brought his eyes to her face, and he saw the telltale flush of color along her cheekbones. With a sharp intake of breath, he caught her chin with his free hand and forced her head back.

There was nowhere to look but into the darkening gray of his eyes. Cami tried to pull her gaze away from him, but she was trapped in the power of his desire. It blazed from him, scorching her, pouring heat through her, filling her with an answering need.

It was like flipping a switch on a time machine. Years disappeared, and it was another summer day. They were young and in love and just beginning to discover the endless dimensions of their passion for each other. She was lost in a mindless haze of sunlight, summer wind, and the scent of field flowers. He was her only reality. Senses spinning under the hot magic of his hungry mouth, she reveled in the feel of the hard, warm strength of his arms and hands cradling her, lifting her, binding her to the taut length of his aroused body.

For long, lovely minutes she feasted on his demanding, teasing, coaxing tongue, aware only of the driving need contracting the muscles deep inside her. She wasn't sure just what brought the first glimmerings of sanity back. Perhaps it was the deeply ingrained female danger signal of impatient male fingers sliding beneath the band of her bikini panties, or it may have been the unfamiliar brushing of his mustache and beard around her lips. Whatever triggered her warning systems, her defenses snapped alert, and her misty mind cleared with a nearly audible whoosh.

She realized several appalling facts all at once. Her hands were clenched in the thickness of Nick's hair, holding his mouth locked with hers. She was half sitting on the edge of the counter in the bathroom, held securely by his arm around her waist, her bare thighs pressed tightly around his thrusting hips. Of overwhelming concern were those enticingly stroking fingers threading their way through her delta of soft curls.

Cami's abrupt transition from melting lover to spitting cat took Nick completely by surprise. In a flurry of arms and legs she shoved him away from her and slid off the counter to her feet, frantically brushing down her crumpled skirt. Eyes blazing almost green with fury, she backed toward the door to the storeroom.

"You... you rotten rake," she sputtered, "and lecher... and... and seducer! You've got one hell of a colossal nerve to come in here and grab me and... and... you have no right! You can just go and... and do nasty things to ducks! And I hope you get a rash!"

Nick flung up both hands in an I-surrender gesture and leaned back against the counter. Any impression of contrition was spoiled, however, by his deep chuckle.

"I wouldn't dare ask you to be more specific, but really, Cami, ducks?" He shook his head slowly, saying mournfully, "The things you wish on me... Come now, firecracker, calm down and straighten yourself out. We have a reservation for seven o'clock, and we really should be moving along."

"I'm not... Oh, all right, but I've got to change," she said, flicking a hand at her wrinkled skirt. "I can't go anywhere looking like this. Why don't you go get acquainted with Jean while I find something else to wear." Noting his questioning look, she added, "We keep some extra clothes here for emergencies."

Nick folded his arms across his chest and settled back more comfortably against the counter. "Why don't I just stay here and talk to you while you change," he offered smoothly.

"No way," she said, opening the door and mustering up a look of long-suffering patience. "Out, Nick. The longer you stall, the later we'll be."

"Spoilsport," he said, strolling past her.

As she closed the door, she heard him singing "You Are Woman, I Am Man" in a baritone croon that would have sent any record company executive scrambling for a pen and a blank contract.

Now that she was alone, Cami quickly regained her usual composure. It was only with the maddening maestro, as she'd once told Jean, that she ever blew her cool and revealed a temperament that was every bit as volatile as his. At the moment her calm efficiency was in the forefront as she rapidly changed into tailored white slacks, a navy-and-lime-striped silk shirt, and her high-heeled white sandals. She flicked a brush through her hair, replaced the lipstick Nick had kissed off, and dashed for the door, snatching up her overstuffed shoulder bag on the way.

She resolutely refused to think about why she was so eager to rejoin her very irritating, very confusing husband. When she left Sea Winds, she'd still had a tiny glimmer of hope that he'd come after her. As the months had gone by, however, with no sign of him, the glimmer had finally faded and died. Yet now, over seven months later, here he was, breathing fire and smoke one minute and kissing her blind stupid the next, pretending he didn't know why she'd left and accusing her of running to another man. Eech! There was no understanding the man!

It was not at all difficult, however, to understand his smug grin when he took in the his-and-hers outfit she was wearing.

"It was all I could find," she muttered, trying unsuccessfully to scowl the grin off his face.

Nick contented himself with a mild "You look very nice."

Jean was busy with a customer, so they merely waved on their way out the door.

2

THEY WERE HALFWAY along Harborside Lane, walking toward Moulton Street, before Cami realized that something was missing.

"Why are we walking? Where's Gavin?" she asked, referring to Nick's longtime valet-chauffeur-bodyguard. She knew that in recent years, since he'd become an increasingly recognized public figure, Nick had developed a preference for moving about by car.

"We don't have far to go—just to Harbor House," he said, naming one of Portland's finest restaurants. "You know, this is—"

"Wait a minute. Don't change the subject. What about Gavin? Never tell me he let you come up here by yourself."

Nick met her questioning look and shrugged. They had both long realized that that first halcyon summer of their marriage would have been very different if Gavin had been with Nick in the Berkshires. With his constant presence, the pace of their courtship would have been closer to a plod than a whirlwind, and they definitely would not have been able to make love wherever and whenever the spirit moved them. Cami had often blessed the Fates that had sent Gavin to England that year to visit his family on the first, and last, long vacation he'd ever taken. That summer had been the happiest time of her marriage, and she'd treasured the memories of it through four long, difficult years.

"Well, did he?" Cami demanded when Nick didn't immediately answer.

"Not exactly. He's here. At least he's down on Cape Elizabeth, where we're staying, but I came up by myself today."

"*You* drove yourself!" squealed Cami, stopping dead in the middle of the sidewalk. "Oh, Lord help us all," she moaned. "Did anyone notify the Portland cops that you were on the loose in a car?"

"Very funny. I'm not *that* bad, and—"

"Oh, yes, you are! Even your mother refuses to get in a car if you're driving. I can't believe Gavin let you take out a car by yourself."

She glanced up at him as they started walking again. She wondered what argument or persuasion he'd used to get past Gavin. Nick was the first to admit that he was one of the world's most absentminded drivers. On the rare occasions when he was in the mood to get behind the wheel, he generally let himself be talked out of it, content to let Gavin, or almost anyone else, chauffeur him. It wasn't that he lacked skill or judgment; when he concentrated on it, he was a very competent driver. And that was the problem: Driving bored him. He either began improvising mind-music or doing mental variations of his repertoire. If there were other people in the car, he'd get so caught up in the conversation that he'd turn around to join in, forgetting completely about watching the traffic or the road.

"There was no problem," said Nick, interrupting her ruminations. "I promised him on a stack of Mozart scores that I'd think of nothing but my driving. He knew I wouldn't get lost because he drove me up here yesterday and made sure I memorized the route."

"Yesterday! What were you . . . Do you mean to tell me . . . Have you been *spying* on me?"

"No, no, of course not," he soothed, snatching his toes away from her stamping foot just in time. As added insurance he grabbed her free hand, which was already balled into a fist. "I've actually been down on Cape Elizabeth for a few days. Once I was really here, in Maine, so close to you and . . . Oh, Cami, suddenly I didn't know what to say or how to approach you. I didn't have any idea why you left, except for that crazy note. What the hell do Chateaubriand and Yankee pot roast have to do with anything?"

Before she had time to do more than open her mouth, he went on with uncharacteristic agitation, "Never mind that. You can explain later. What I'm trying to say is that it took me a couple of days to bring myself to . . . I didn't know whether to go to your apartment or just walk into the shop. I finally decided to at least go to the shop and see . . . Well, I did yesterday . . . looked in from the sidewalk, that is, and you weren't there, so I wandered around this Port place for a while and . . ."

His voice trailed off as Cami started laughing. "What's so funny?" he growled.

"You . . . you . . ." she sputtered, choking back the rising giggles. "I just can't imagine *you* being nervous about *anything!*"

"Yes . . . well . . . there's a first time for everything, and I seem to be having a hell of a lot of them with you." Nick finally became aware of the sidelong looks they were receiving from passersby. "This isn't the best place to discuss this." He started down Moulton

Street toward the harborfront. "You can tell me about this area on the way. Some of these old buildings are fascinating."

Although she would have preferred exploring this inexplicable lapse in her husband's heretofore supreme self-confidence, Cami reluctantly agreed that a busy sidewalk was not the best place for an in-depth analysis. She acquiesced, therefore, to Nick's request and discussed the Old Port Exchange, one of the largest privately funded restoration projects in the country, which comprised several square blocks reaching back from the harbor toward the center of the city. Once a derelict and nearly abandoned area of Portland, the blocks of late-nineteenth-century granite and brick buildings now housed a wide variety of craft and antique shops, boutiques, galleries, and the like. The area had also become the "in" place for the younger professionals in the city to set up their offices and practices.

Nick was intrigued with the late Victorian architectural whimsies that decorated some of the buildings. Cami was less intrigued with the brick sidewalks, which lent atmosphere but were a hazard when walking in heels. Enjoying the novelty of Cami's voluntarily clinging to his arm, Nick sighed regretfully when they reached the restaurant.

Cami had too much past experience with the de Conti method of doing things to be surprised when they were led to one of the coveted window tables. Her only question was, "When did you arrange this?"

"This afternoon while I was wandering around killing time." Nick scanned the dining room and added, "Nice. Hope the food's as good as its reputation."

"It's terrific," Cami assured him. "Jean and I come here for lunch once in a while. I love the atmosphere."

She looked around at the gleam of polished brass

and the soft glow of old, well-cared-for oak. The expanse of the big room was reduced to cozy areas by the clever placement of paneled screens and sweeps of rich burgundy velvet suspended from thick, waist-high brass rails. Strategically placed large, lush floor plants also contributed to a feeling of privacy. The long harborside wall was lined with huge Venetian windows, and now, in early evening, the fading sunlight pouring in shimmered faintly from the reflection of the last flashing ripples across the water.

"You could easily eat here three times a day if you really wanted to." Nick's mildly voiced comment brought her attention back to him.

"They don't do breakfasts," she said absently, trying to read his expression through the mass of facial hair.

Cami noted the challenge in his eyes and knew that he was remembering all their arguments about the extravagant monthly allowance he had insisted on allotting to her shortly after their marriage. She had never liked the idea of being given an allowance. Something about it made her feel like a dependent child or a kept woman. In her world, husbands and wives pooled their resources and had joint accounts. She remembered his blistering reply to her compromise proposal that he reduce her allowance to an amount that matched her trust income. *That* was the argument that had ended with flying pots, a tender bottom, and a night-long reconciliation.

"That's a very interesting expression. Just what are you remembering?"

Cami could feel the blush spreading up from her neck. She knew from the husky amusement in his voice that he'd probably guessed at her train of thought. A quick look at his face and she was sure from the darkening of his knowing eyes that he was also remembering how his imaginative efforts to soothe her smarting rear had led to one of their wildest nights of lovemaking.

She stared out the window, hardly aware of the busy harbor scene spread out in front of her, as she tried to regain her composure.

"Cami?"

She turned back to Nick with what she hoped was an expression of friendly interest. Something about his twitching mustache told her that she wasn't entirely successful.

"All right, Nick. I'm sure you find it all no end amusing. At least I'm honest enough to admit that the *one* thing that stayed right with our marriage was the sex. I won't play your dumb games anymore by pretending that everything's basically fine except for some minor misunderstandings. Those—"

She broke off as the wine steward arrived, and waited impatiently as he and Nick went through their ritual. Catching the look he flicked her way, she realized that Nick was deliberately prolonging the little ceremony of sniffing the cork and tasting the vintage wine.

At last the steward left, and Nick held his glass out toward her. "A toast, *cara?*"

Cami's expression was definitely mutinous as she picked up her glass and growled, "To what?"

"To us, of course," he said softly as he touched his glass to hers. He took a sip of the white wine, watching her as she hesitated. "Drink up, my stubborn darling," he coaxed, reaching across the table and guiding her glass to her mouth. "There is stiil an 'us.' If I didn't believe that, I wouldn't have gone through all the frustration and soul-searching of the past few months."

"Oh" was all Cami could manage as she sought frantically to analyze that last statement. Frustration was understandable. Nick gave beautiful demonstrations of frustration every time his plans or schedules were disrupted or his will was thwarted. However, soul-searching had not been one of his usual practices. It would imply that he had made a mistake in judgment or in handling a personal relationship, and, as Cami well knew, Nick did not admit to human fallibility. She wasn't quite ready for soul-searchings on an empty stomach, but those frustrations . . .

While she worked out an approach, Cami sipped her wine and watched the flexing of muscles and tendons in Nick's hands as he coated thin wheat crackers with the restaurant's famous cheese spread. She firmly subdued the rising memories of those magical hands stroking and exploring her eager body. *Talk about frustrations! This will never do. At least, not yet.*

"Cami? Aren't you going to have some of this? It's terrific. I don't suppose you know what's in it, do you?"

She took the cracker he was offering and savored a bite. "It's the most closely guarded secret in town, but I heard," she whispered, suddenly lighthearted as she leaned forward with a teasing smile, "that it includes at least four kinds of cheese and two or three varieties of ground nuts. Beyond that, nobody knows."

White teeth flashed through the dark forest of beard and mustache as Nick chuckled. "I wonder which holds the most appeal: the fact that it's delicious or the fun of trying to solve a mystery."

"Speaking of mysteries," said Cami, never one to pass up a golden opportunity, "what were all those frustrations you mentioned a few minutes ago?"

"What kind of a dumb question is that?" Nick snapped, managing with obvious effort to keep his voice down. "How did you think I was going to feel, coming home after a grueling six-week tour in Aus-

tralia and New Zealand and finding you gone, with
no explanation and no word as to when you'd be back
or even where you were? And don't, please, tell me
you left a note. I figured out more from the fact that
you'd left everything I'd given you—your ring, your
jewelry, and all your clothes."

"I—"

"That note you left for Mother wasn't much more
informative: 'Don't worry. I've gone to visit relatives.' Some visit. By the time I got back you'd been
gone almost four weeks, and no one had heard a word
from you. Since the only relatives I knew of were
your aunt and uncle, I called them, only to discover
that they didn't know where you were, either."

"Nick, after all they'd done for me, I couldn't ask
them—"

"Don't you understand, Cami? There it was, two
days before Thanksgiving—a major family holiday—
and I didn't have a clue as to where my wife was,
whether she was sick and alone someplace, or even
if she was alive. No, don't interrupt. Now that I've
started, let me get it out. I'm sure you believed you
had a good reason for leaving like that, but did you
give any thought to how I was going to feel, not
knowing if you were alive or dead? The last time I
saw you, you were as thin as a rake, you didn't have
a trace of color in your face, your eyes were sunk in
dark circles, and you were in the depths of a severe
depression. During the two whole months I'd been
home you wouldn't talk to me or even stay in the
same room with me. I know you were upset about the
miscarriage, especially since it was the second time
and I hadn't been with you through either one. If only
someone had called me, I would have canceled the
Italian concerts and come home. I could have been
with you."

"You'd have canceled a concert?"

"Oh, Cami, what kind of a man do you think I am? Don't you know how close I came to canceling the whole Australian tour? I didn't want to leave you when you looked so sick and were so upset, but Mother insisted that women recovered faster on their own, that it was natural for you to blame me for putting you through the anguish, and that you'd do much better if I were out of sight for a while. So I went on the tour and—"

"Is that what she told you? And you believed her? Oh, Lord, and you call *me* dumb? I needed you, Nick. I've never needed anyone so much in my whole life. I lay in that hospital bed and waited for you to come through the door and...you didn't come and didn't come, and then Lucianna...your mother said that you...she said she'd talked to you, and you were too angry and upset with me to...that you didn't even want to talk to me until you'd calmed down. She said you were very disappointed in me, that if you'd known in the beginning that I couldn't have children—"

"*No!*"

Cami stared as Nick's hand clamped tightly over hers, stilling her fingers, which had been nervously shredding the crackers into a pile of crumbs.

"I never said any of that, Cami." He leaned over the table, his eyes holding hers with an almost frightening intensity, his voice raspy with shocked disbelief. "My Lord, what was Mother thinking of to tell you—Cami, I swear I didn't know anything about the miscarriage until Gavin met my flight from Rome and told me. I was furious; I couldn't believe that everyone had kept it a secret from me for almost two weeks. I couldn't wait to get home, and then, before I even got in the front door, Mother met me and told me you were distraught and still very weak, and that it would be best not to say too much about the baby."

Cami stared at him with dawning hope. Now, at long last, maybe he was beginning to believe what she'd tried so many times to tell him about how his mother really felt about her and their marriage. Was he also ready to believe the truth about his marvelous manager, Arthur Rossman, and the part he'd played in stirring up distrust and misunderstanding between them?

"Nick?"

"Wait. Let me think about all this for a few minutes. We'll have another glass of wine while they start our dinner."

He signaled to the waiter, who had apparently been keeping an eye on them, since he nodded an acknowledgment and disappeared in the direction of the kitchen. Nick refilled their wineglasses from the bottle that had been left chilling next to the table, and leaned back in his chair, his elbow propped on the padded arm as he took occasional sips of wine. He met Cami's questioning eyes and then slowly, unable to resist the temptation any longer, he let his gaze drift down over her firm, high breasts and slim torso. When he brought his eyes back up to hers, he had to smile at the flush of color staining her cheeks.

"You've gained back most of the weight you lost, haven't you? You look much better—except, of course, for that haircut," he added hastily.

His smile widened to a grin as he saw the sparks flare in her eyes, but then she laughed at him and chided, "You'll just have to get used to it."

He sobered suddenly and leaned forward, reaching across the table to lay the palm of his hand gently against her cheek.

"Your eyes are laughing," he said softly. "Do you

know how long it's been since I've seen them do that? Do you remember the first time I called you my Lady Laughing Eyes?"

"Oh, yes," she whispered, leaning her cheek against his cradling hand, her eyes caught by his in a web of shared memories.

Nick and Cami stared at each other with remembering gazes and a growing assurance that perhaps, at last, they could put right what had gone so wrong with their marriage.

"That first summer in the Berkshires was so good, and we were so close . . . and then I took you home, and it all started to fall apart." Nick's voice held a rare note of uncertainty. "I'm still not sure I understand just what—"

He broke off as the waiter arrived with their appetizers. When Cami looked at him questioningly, Nick explained, "I looked over the menu when I stopped by to make a reservation, and I decided to surprise you with a special dinner."

"If this is as good as it looks, I just might forgive you for that cracked elbow," Cami teased as she explored the delicious-smelling concoction of snails nested in artichoke bottoms and drenched in garlic butter. "Ummmm . . . this is incredible. Here, try some," she offered, transferring a sampling to the edge of Nick's plate.

She was busy eyeing the tall parfait glass in front of him and didn't notice his satisfied look as she instinctively reverted to their old habit of sharing.

"And I suppose you want some of this," sighed Nick with mock resignation.

She smiled and drawled, "Well, it does look rather fascinating, and so colorful. What is it? Is that *green* mayonnaise?"

"It's a shrimp parfait. It's got . . . let's see . . . chunks of shrimp, shredded lettuce, pimiento strips, sieved hard-boiled eggs, capers, and, yes, that's green mayonnaise. They do it with herbs and whatnot. Here, open your mouth," he commanded, holding a forkful of the mixture two inches from her lips.

She obeyed automatically before the intimacy of what they were doing occurred to her. Startled, she raised her eyes to his and found him watching her with heart-melting tenderness.

"It's all right, *cara*," he said softly. "Let's just enjoy our dinner for now. We can get back to unknotting our tangled web later."

"Oh, Nick, do you really think we can?"

"Of course we can—now that we've finally started talking to each other again."

"That's not fair," she protested. "I've always tried to talk to you. You just weren't listening before."

"Well, my sweet elf, disappearing on me for over seven months was positively guaranteed to get my undivided attention. Now I'm listening."

"That isn't why I—"

"Not now. Later, after dinner, we'll talk about it all, although I think I'm beginning to get the picture. But right now, why don't you tell me about your shop."

Cami hesitated for a few seconds, her mind filled with a rapidly flickering montage of half-finished conversations, uncompleted scenes, yelling arguments, and Nick's closed expression and his voice repeating endlessly, "Cami, I know what's best." She looked at him intently, searching for the truth, and with a relieved sigh realized that he was completely sincere. At last, he was ready to listen and believe.

"All right, Nick, we'll save it all for later. What do you want to know about old kitchen thingamabobs?"

* * *

It was deep twilight by the time they left Harbor House and started ambling back toward Harborside Lane. The streetlights spaced along the brick sidewalks were copies of old gas lamps, and they added a warm ambience to the soft June evening. A light breeze was drifting off the harbor, bringing a salt tang to blend with the sweet scents from the flowers in the many windowboxes and the brick planters along the walks.

After they had strolled for a few minutes in companionable silence, Cami said softly, "I had given up hope, you know, that you'd try to find me. It was so long and—"

"No, my wayward darling. There was no question about whether I'd come after you. It was a matter of, first, finding you—which took much longer than I expected—and, second, arranging the how and when."

Nick let go of her hand and slipped his arm around her shoulders, giving her a quick, tight hug as he felt her arm slide around his waist. Without conscious thought, they adjusted their steps to the same rhythm.

"In all those arguments we had," he continued, "you were forever accusing me of being arrogant and selfish, of not caring about how you felt. During these months, waiting for the investigator to find you, I've had endless hours to think about us, about you, about how things could have gotten so bad between us that you'd leave me."

He stopped and turned her to face him, tipping her head back with his free hand so she'd have to meet his eyes. "Do you know what I discovered?"

"What?" she whispered, mesmerized by the intensity of his gaze.

"That much of what you said was true, and that I wanted nothing so much as the chance to make it all up to you, to tell you how much I love you and how much I want us to be as happy and as close as we were in those first weeks we were married."

"Oh, Nick..."

He started them walking again. "Once I knew where you were and what you were doing, I realized that I couldn't just come crashing in and drag you back home. We needed time to be alone together, to sort out all the problems, and to find our way back to each other. It wasn't something that could be done in a few days, either. So I exercised my limited patience—with great difficulty, believe me—and fulfilled a commitment to teach several master classes in New York in May, while I forced Arthur to get me out of everything else for the next three months."

"Three months! You're taking the whole summer off?"

"June, July, and August. And we're spending it here."

"Here?" she questioned cautiously. As amazed as she was at his revelations, she didn't believe for a moment that he'd undergone a complete personality change. Just because he was willing to admit that he'd been arrogant didn't necessarily mean that he wouldn't continue to be. It would be wiser, she decided, to hear his plans before she got too excited.

"In Maine. On Cape Elizabeth, to be exact. The Cattons have lent us their house while they're in Europe for the summer. It's very quiet and peaceful, right on the coast, about forty-five minutes from here. They have a private beach and—"

"But, Nick, I can't just take off for the summer. I—"

"Yes, yes, I know about the shop and—" He broke off and glanced around, realizing that they had stopped in front of the shop. "Where's your car? We'll go home and continue this in comfort."

"Across the street in that little parking lot. Home,

where? It's getting late, Nick, and I've got to be up early."

"Home with me, of course," he answered, drawing her across the street after him. "I'll drive you in in the morning and pick up my car, and then—"

"Wait a minute, general," she yelped, bracing her feet and pulling him to a halt at the edge of the parking lot. "Stop organizing me. I'm not going to the Cape tonight or staying overnight with you. At least not yet. I mean—We've got a lot of sorting out to do before we get to—Oh, damn. Listen, Nick, I want to go home—my home—and think about all this and—"

"Fine," he said cheerfully. "I'll drive you to your place."

"And then how will you get home?" she asked suspiciously. "Where's your car? Are you planning something sneaky?"

"Now, *cara,* what could I be planning? My car's in the parking garage," he said blandly, waving a hand vaguely in the air. "I can call a cab from your place."

He looked around the small parking lot that contained only—"*A truck?*" he asked disbelievingly.

"What's wrong with my truck?" Cami demanded, striding toward the sporty Ford Ranger pickup, custom-painted in pale blue with bands of turquoise and pine green.

On the door panel, Nick could just make out a small silhouette of a cast-iron stove and "Grandma's Kitchen" in discreet black soutache lettering.

"It's very practical, and I can write it off as a company vehicle," she muttered as she dug through her shoulder bag for her keys. Nick reached for them as she pulled them out, but Cami quickly whipped her hand behind her back.

"No way, you bearded, menace," she said, laughing. "I like my truck the way it is—without dents, dangling bumpers, or unsightly gouges."

"So be it, oh ye of little faith," he conceded as he walked around to the far side and waited for her to reach across and unlock the door.

Cami had a fleeting, malicious thought as to what Lucianna would say if she could see her precious son riding in a truck. Her ideas on proper motor vehicles were limited to chauffeur-driven limousines or Italian sports jobs in the $40,000-and-up range.

"This isn't bad," Nick said, adjusting the seat to accommodate his long legs. "Bucket seats, carpeting, padded dash, cassette player. I didn't know trucks were so fancy."

Cami gave him a mocking glance as she pulled out of the parking lot. "When have you ever been in a truck before?"

They bantered back and forth during the few minutes' drive, and Cami found herself once again relaxing with the return of their old easy familiarity. She was rather sorry the ride was so short.

Nick peered out the window, checking his memory of the route Gavin had driven him over yesterday. Things looked different at night, and he wanted to be sure he could return alone if necessary. He was pleased when he recognized the turn onto the Eastern Promenade, a wide road that ran for more than a mile along the perimeter of a high rise of land above Casco Bay, and that was bordered on the seaward side by a sixty-eight-acre park. The landward side of the Promenade was lined with wide, sloping lawns fronting a fascinating assortment of huge frame houses, most of which had been built in the late 1800s.

"This place is incredible," he said as Cami turned off the Promenade into the driveway beside a massive, sprawling, late-Victorian house. "It must have been designed by a cross-eyed carpenter with delusions of grandeur. How many rooms are there?"

Cami pulled the truck in beside several other vehicles in a small parking area at the rear of the house. "I'm not quite sure," she said, chuckling, as they got out of the truck. "Come this way. I'm on the bay side. It depends on what you're counting as a room. For instance, you can get into the cupola through a trap door, and there's a window seat that goes all around, so is it a room or not? Do you count a pantry big enough to waltz in as a room or as part of the kitchen?"

"I get the picture," he said, peering up at what he could see of the house in the dark. "What do you call a glassed-in sun porch, and how do you count large rooms that have been partitioned into smaller ones?"

"You can understand, then, why the answer to your question is that there are between twenty-five and forty rooms," she said over her shoulder, leading the way along a flower-bordered walk that curved gracefully across the wide lawn at the side of the house.

Nick turned his face toward the strong breeze, which carried the tangy scents of the sea, and stopped for a moment to search for a sight of the water that he knew was close by.

"What are those lights, Cami? Boats?"

She turned back and moved up beside him, following the direction of his pointing finger. "Some of them probably are, but most of them are on the nearby islands. Come on in," she invited, turning back toward the house. "We'll go up to the turret porch. You'll have a much better—What's the matter?"

She spun around at the sound of a strangled oath, which was immediately followed by a burst of laughter, and saw Nick staring up at the house. Remembering her own stunned reaction when she first saw this side of the building, she joined in his laughter.

"Wild, isn't it? Do you believe how many architectural froufrous they managed to cram into . . . what, eighty, ninety feet? . . . however long the side of the house is?"

"Unbelievable," murmured Nick as he took in the ells, bays—both circular and multisided—oddly shaped verandas and porches, gables, and other imaginative projections encrusting the side and roof of the building.

The walk Cami had been following led to a screened porch, angled between a rare, clear fifteen-foot stretch of the main wall and the twelve-foot flat portion of a projecting ell. Nick's fascinated eyes, however, were on the two-story octagonal bay that seemed to blossom forth from the outer corner of the ell. He tipped his head back for a better view of the whimsical structure topping the bay, its white paint glowing in the moonlight making it look as if it had been spun of sugar icing.

"What in the world is that?"

"That's my eyrie. Isn't it terrific?" Cami gazed proudly up at the white latticework ringing the lower part of the turret and the delicate-looking but sturdy pillars rising above the waist-high railing every few feet to support the domed roof.

It's at least three stories up," said Nick. "I'll grant you a fantastic view, but it looks as if it would blow away in a strong wind."

"Uh-uh. It's been up there almost a hundred years. Come on. I'll show you," she urged, grabbing his hand and tugging him after her along the walk. "My 'sky seat' is the reason I took this crazy apartment, despite its weird bathroom and a kitchen designed by and for giants."

She laughed up at him and lilted, "Oh, Nick, this is really going to be an eye-opener for you. You have no idea how normal people live."

He gave her a disbelieving look and motioned toward the house. "You call *this* normal? Now who's got bats in her attic?"

"Well, it's a lot more normal than living in a thirty-room museum like Sea Winds and tripping over guards and servants every time you turn around," Cami muttered as she pushed open the screen door to the porch.

Nick prudently decided to let that one pass and searched for a change of subject. "Don't you have a light out here?" he gasped as he stubbed his toe on a solid brass umbrella stand, which he hadn't seen in the unrelieved darkness of the porch.

"Shhh. You'll wake someone up." Nick could just make out her face as she leaned toward him to continue whispering, "A lot of these people go to bed early."

He glanced around at the few windows in sight, noting that most of them were dark. Only two showed a dim glow of light behind tightly drawn shades. Turning back to Cami, he was suddenly aware of the stillness of the night, the privacy of the deeply shadowed porch, and the evocative scent of lilac drifting up from her hair. It was more than he could stand. He'd really intended to accede to her wishes about keeping things cool until they could discuss their problems, but—

"Carissima," he whispered, bending to press his face into her curls as his arms closed around her and pulled her up against the full length of his warm, hard body.

Taken off guard, Cami's mind had no time to grasp control of her instincts. At the first touch of Nick's hands on her back, her arms slid up across his shoulders and wound around his neck. The familiar cadence of Italian love-talk whispered in her ear brought her face up, and she felt the strange, soft brush of his beard across her sensitive skin as she molded her mouth to his, igniting fires in both of them that had been banked for far too long.

They swayed, locked tightly together, for long mo-

ments, and it was only Nick's muttered curse as he
tried to remove her shoulder bag that snapped Cami
back to reality. She brought her hands down to his
chest, pushing firmly against him as she dropped back
onto her heels.

"No," she growled. "You know where this is going
to lead, dammit, and we're going to talk first. Lots
of talk, Nick."

He reluctantly let her go, protesting, "But, *cara,*
what's wrong with talking in bed? Afterward. We
could—"

"No, no, no." Cami fumbled for her keys in the
side pocket of her bag, trying at the same time to get
her breathing back under control. Her emphatic nos
were aimed at herself as much as at Nick. Her hands
were shaking, her knees were melting, and she could
feel the flush of arousal pulsing over every inch of
her skin. It took all of her hard-won determination to
keep from turning back into the passionate promise
of his arms.

"Nick, you agreed," she insisted as she finally got
the door open and stepped into the hall. She flipped
a switch, flooding the foyer with light, and dropped
her bag on the marble-topped console.

"Hmmmm. Did I?" he murmured as he moved
behind her and slid his eager hands around her small
waist.

"Close enough," she chided, removing herself from
his grasp and grabbing one of his hands. She started
for the stairs, tugging him determinedly after her.
"Come along, you impossible Lothario, and see the
view from the turret. Maybe the sea breezes will cool
you down."

"Don't count on it," he murmured with a soft
chuckle as he followed her up the stairs.

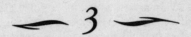

3

"OH, MY STARS... and garters... I don't believe we ...did this... that..." Cami moaned between pants as she tried to get her breath back.

Reality was returning with unwelcome speed and clarity. Between one gasping breath and the next, she was suddenly, appallingly aware of the hot hardness of Nick's body pressed tightly against hers, held there by the force of her bare legs locked around his hips and the stranglehold of her arms around his neck. She buried her face deeper into the curve of his neck, mortified beyond further words as her nerve endings transmitted more dismaying news. Except for her blouse and bra, both open and pushed to her sides, she was naked, her bare breasts and belly crushed against the thick furring of Nick's body hair. She could feel the pressure of his pelvis as he held himself locked inside her, absorbing the tiny aftershocks of her climax. The muscles of his spread legs were taut and trembling with the strain of bracing himself against the railing to keep them upright, while his large warm hands firmly cupped her bottom to balance her on—

"Oh, my Lord!" Cami squealed. "Let me down, Nick! Nick! Get me off here! My bottom is—Anybody could look up here and see—Ohhhh," she moaned, near tears, "how would I explain *this* to my landlady? Or anyone else? What—"

"Calm down, *cara,*" chided Nick with an unmistakable thread of laughter in his voice. He pressed his cheek against the top of her head and looked over her shoulder. A quick scan of the yard and the few shaded windows with a view of the turret porch assured him that they were unobserved. "No one can see anything, even if they should look up here, and why would they anyhow? It's dark and—"

Cami lifted her head and glared at him. "My bare butt is hanging over this railing and probably glowing like a rising moon and—"

"And I have it covered with my hands. Watch it! Don't lean back, you little idiot, or you'll have us both tumbling off here. Now what are you doing?"

Cami had finally thought to unlock her ankles and let her legs drop from around Nick's hips, but his continued closeness stopped her from sliding down off the railing. She braced her hands against his hipbones, trying futilely to push him away from her. She was also trying, with equal futility, not to think about what had just happened.

"Dominic de Conti, will you please, please let me down from here? I—We—Oh, dammit!"

"How things have changed," Nick said with a particularly plaintive sigh. "You used to like to stay in my arms afterward while we stroked each other and— All right, all right! Stop wiggling. I'll put you down."

He slid his hands up to her waist and lifted her off the railing. As soon as her feet touched the floor, she leaped for the center of the porch, well out of sight of anything other than a nosy bird.

There was sufficient light from the half-moon for her to see more than she wanted to. Her shoes, slacks, and panties and Nick's shirt were strewn across the floor near the railing. His shoes were still on his feet, and she reluctantly raised her eyes from them to take in the rest of him.

"Blast!" she exploded, flinging her arms wide. "Look at us! We look like an X-rated movie!"

Nick threw back his head with a shout of laughter and matched her arm-flinging gesture. It gave her an unobstructed view of his lean, nearly naked body. She tried to look away but couldn't. The moonlight silvered the tanned skin stretched tautly over the sinews of his bare shoulders and arms, providing a sharp contrast to the darkness of the mat of curling hair covering his chest and narrowing down across his stomach to spread out into a soft thicket covering his groin. Her gaze became fixed, and she felt a hot melting in her belly as she realized just why men liked their women to wear at least a hint of a garment over their nakedness.

The least he could do is pull up those damn bitty French briefs . . . and his jeans, not stand there flaunting his—Oh, no! Not again. Not here. Blast him anyhow; I didn't want to go this far this soon. We haven't settled anything or discussed—

"Nick, don't you dare! Stay right where you are, and for heaven's sake, pull up your pants! We've got a lot of talking to do before—Oww . . . oooo, that smarts! Ouch!"

"What's the matter?" Nick demanded, quickly covering himself and zipping his jeans as he stepped toward Cami. He reached to grasp her shoulders and still her frantic squirming. "Cami, tell me what's wrong."

"Splinters!" she snarled, brushing her fingers lightly over her tender bottom. "That railing was full of splinters! I didn't feel them until I tried to move."

"Well, then, stand still," said Nick, trying desperately to hold back his laughter. It really wasn't funny, he thought. They were probably painful . . . but leave it to his Cami to turn a fantastic moment of intense passion into farce.

"I can't stand still," she wailed. "They hurt. And how am I going to get dressed and get down those stairs? Oh, good Lord," she breathed, grabbing his arms and staring up at him in horror. "How am I going to get them out? Oh, Nick, I can't, simply can't go waltzing into the emergency room and tell them I have a butt full of splinters! How would I explain that? They'd all fall over in hysterics. They'd—"

"Cami, Cami, *cara,* calm down. You don't have to explain anything to anybody. I'll take them out."

"You! But—"

"Yes, me. I'm not as helpless as you seem to think. Well, really, how difficult can it be to pull out a few slivers?"

"A few! It feels like hundreds. And it's too embarrassing. I'll call Jean and—"

"Don't be ridiculous," he sighed in exasperation. "You can't call Jean out at this time of night. Are you forgetting how close an acquaintance I have with your delightful derriere? Although I must admit I've never seen it bristling with splinters."

"Stop laughing at me, you . . . you caveman. If you hadn't lost control of—"

"Hah! Who was climbing me like a hungry cat scrambling up a tree after a tasty bird? Who pulled off my shirt? Who was swearing at my beard because she couldn't find my mouth? Who—"

"I don't want to discuss it," she stated, pulling her

shirt closed in belated modesty and trying to ignore the fact that she was naked from hips to toes.

"You're right. We've had enough discussion. It's time to de-splinter you."

Before she realized his intention, Nick lunged for her and tossed her over his shoulder. Oblivious to both her outraged sputterings and the small fists hammering at his back, he wove a path through the scattered porch furniture, heading toward the stairs.

"Cami? You awake?"

"Mmmmm... sort of."

"How do you feel now?"

"As if I'd sat on a bed of nails. Are you sure you disinfected the... ah, area... thoroughly?"

"Yes, but I'm not sure you shouldn't have a shot or something, just to be safe."

"It's not necessary. Since we handle so much rusty metal and spend so much time in grubby old barns, Jean and I always have our anti-tetanus boosters up to date."

"What about—"

"Nick, I'm fine. Go to sleep."

"Cami?"

"Now what?"

"Where did you get this bed? Did it come with the place?"

"No, I bought it. Why? What's wrong with it?"

"Nothing, *cara,* not a thing."

"Good. Now can I go to sleep?"

"It's not very big, is it?"

"It's a standard double."

"Oh."

"It's plenty big enough for me."

"Yes, well, you're elf-sized. It's rather cramped for a normal person, isn't it?"

"Nick, believe me, thousands—no, millions—of couples sleep in beds this size every night, and they manage just fine."

"No wonder there are so many divorces—all those people trying to sleep all bent up."

"What are you muttering about?"

"Nothing, *cara*. Why don't you go to sleep?"

"That's what I've been trying to do for—"

"If you move over here, I'll rub your back."

"I'm in no condition for one of your backrubs. You know where that leads."

"Mmmmm. My own Lady Laughing Eyes, it's been seven very long months. And even before that, it had been—"

"Not on your nellie, Nick. Not until we've sorted out a few misunderstandings and decided—"

"You weren't objecting a few minutes ago. In fact, you were downright eager."

"Dammit, you took me by surprise. And there was all that soupy moonlight and those soft breezes, and I never said we weren't dynamite together. Once you started kissing me...well...but there's more to marriage than sex."

"Don't you think—"

"I think we spent too much time either yelling at each other or making love, and not enough time communicating. Communicating, Nick, means talking, discussing, planning, exchanging ideas and thoughts, and coming to an agreement on some basics."

"All right, let's communicate. No, love, don't pull away. At least let me hold your hand. You don't look very comfortable all curled up like that."

"I'm not, but you're taking up three-fourths of the bed."

"I can't straighten out any other way. Here, move over beside me and stretch out."

"But—"

"Come on, Cami. Is there a rule that you can only lie in one direction? There, isn't that better?"

"And we're going to talk like this?"

"Promise. Where do you want to start?"

"Are you really going to listen this time, Nick?"

"Yes, *cara,* I'm really going to listen."

"And believe me?"

"I'll believe you."

"Even if it's about your mother?"

"Yes. Obviously Mother's been... meddling."

"That's putting it mildly. And Rossman?"

"Arthur? What's he got to do with this?"

"Oh, Nick, how blind can you be? Your mother and Arthur Rossman started concocting their nasty little plot from the day you brought me to Sea Winds."

"Now wait a minute. I was there. My mother welcomed you and—"

"Right. While you were there. But there were hours on end when you were practicing or conferring with Rossman, and you had no idea of the things your mother and sisters were saying to me. They wasted no time letting me know how totally unsuitable I was to be a de Conti wife. My clothes were wrong, my hair was wrong, my accent was wrong, my manners were wrong. My attitudes were drearily middle class, my ethics naive, and my cultural tastes akin to those of Neanderthal woman."

"Cami!"

"It's not funny. You simply don't realize how much can be said with a raised eyebrow or an exasperated look."

"Are you sure you didn't imagine slights where there weren't any simply because you felt insecure? After all, it was a big change from your previous life and—"

"No, Nick, I didn't imagine anything. It wasn't all looks and innuendos, you know. They, especially your mother, came right out and said things very clearly. And I wasn't insecure, at least not in the beginning. Sure, it was a different way of life, and one I'd had no experience with. But I've always been a quick study, and I assumed I'd have you to back me up."

"I did try to help you, *cara*."

"Oh, yes, by telling me to listen to your mother and sisters. What about the times I tried to tell you that your family didn't want me there and that your mother was determined to break us up? You wouldn't listen to a word against them, but you believed every negative thing they said about me."

"I didn't take their comments as negative. I merely thought they were pointing out the problems you were having in adjusting."

"I could have explained my own problems if I could ever have gotten near you. You were always either off somewhere or shut up in the music room practicing."

"Did you resent my music?"

"No! Never! That was another of Lucianna's poisoned darts. Oh, Nick, how can I get through to you how utterly frustrating it all was? All the little things that by themselves were unimportant—nothing more than gnat's nips—but put together and piled up higher and higher every day, they became a solid wall of antagonism and misunderstanding. Don't you see? Your mother and Rossman were feeding you a constant diet of hints, suggestions, and outright lies."

"Why didn't you—"

"Talk to you? I tried, Nick. When were we ever left alone except at night when we went to bed? Tell me that you were willing to talk then. Go ahead, tell me. You know—"

"All right, *cara,* I'll agree that I didn't want to spend our nights discussing your problems with—"

"And how many nights were there? I figured it out not long ago. In four years you averaged less than four months per year at home. The rest of the time you were either on tour or off teaching master classes somewhere. How was I supposed to talk to you then?"

"I called you countless times from all over the world, but you were hardly ever there. From what Mother said, you were finding plenty to do, and yet—"

"In the first place, your mother lied. Yes, Nick, *lied!* Almost every time she said I was out, I wasn't. I was somewhere in the house, and she simply didn't call me to the phone. When I asked her why, she always said you'd been in a hurry and couldn't wait for me to get there."

"You never—"

"Yes, I did. You were too busy yelling at me about never being around when you called to listen to a word I was saying. Why did you think I wanted a separate phone line in our sitting room?"

"Mother said—"

"I don't want to hear it! She just—"

"Stop bouncing, Cami."

". . . wanted to keep control of my phone calls. She used to listen in on an extension—"

"My mother would never—"

". . . whenever she knew I was talking to a friend. Furthermore, on the rare occasions when I did get to talk to you, she either stayed on the extension or hovered at my shoulder the whole time. What was I supposed to say to you with her listening to every word?"

"Cami . . ."

"We could have been together, Nick. At least, a lot more than we were. I'd have given anything to have gone on tour with you. You wouldn't even discuss it. You simply informed me that you were going and I was staying."

"Arthur felt—"

"Oh, yes, Arthur. Arthur, dear thoughtful Arthur, convinced you that I'd be bored spending so much time alone in strange places. Well, let me tell you, love, they couldn't have been any stranger than Sea Winds—or any more boring."

"It's true, though, that you would have been alone a great deal while I was—"

"Nick, you idiot, I was a history major. I've always wanted to travel and see all the places I'd learned about. I could have taken day tours when you were practicing, or visited museums, or done a hundred different things. I would *not* have been bored!"

"But Arthur...and Mother...they were so sure—"

"They were sure that if we spent enough time together, I'd throw a king-sized monkey wrench into the middle of their plans."

"What are you talking about?"

"Nick, five years ago you were already at the top. You were considered one of the few truly brilliant classical pianists of this century, and you were only twenty-eight, with years of concerts, recordings, and who knows what ahead of you. Your mother and Rossman had been carefully following a master plan for your career, and for years they had made sure that nothing interfered with it."

"You make it sound as if I don't have a mind of my own."

"Of course you do, but you know you agreed with all their ideas. Why not? You didn't have any worries about the things normal people have to consider. They wrapped you in a comfortable cocoon. Did you ever have to hunt for a clean shirt, or make a plane reservation, or think about what to eat for breakfast, or decide where to spend a vacation? No. As far as Rossman and your family were concerned, the most important thing was your tremendous talent, and nothing was allowed to interfere with developing it and sharing it with an appreciative public."

"What's wrong with that?"

"Nothing, Nick. I agree with much of it. Not all of it, but a lot. However, they didn't consider the possibility that you'd fall in love with and marry a woman who might not be willing to sacrifice a close and loving relationship for the sake of their plans for your career."

"I don't understand what you're getting at, Cami."

"Think about the *ifs*, Nick. *If* no one had convinced you I'd be bored on tour, you'd have taken me with you. *If* I'd had enough time alone with you, I'd have convinced you that we needed the privacy of our own house. *If* these people hadn't connived to keep us as far apart and as much at odds as possible, we'd have developed a deep and trusting relationship."

"All right, Cami, I can see that part, but—"

"Now then, just consider what might have happened. With our own home and without anyone to orchestrate our private time for us, you would have learned just how wonderful that deep and trusting relationship could be. Suppose you decided that you didn't want to spend eight out of twelve months touring the world on a grueling concert schedule. After all, that kind of intensive exposure isn't necessary anymore. Suppose you decided that, say, two tours a year of six to eight weeks each would be enough to satisfy your public, along with your recordings, of course, and perhaps an occasional guest appearance or TV special. That would give you much more time at home with your wife and children—"

"But you—"

"I'll get to that in a minute. It would also give you time to compose, which I know you want to do."

"And why do you think Mother and Arthur would object to any of that?"

"Oh, Nick, in some ways you are unbelievably...innocent. How does Arthur make his money? Hmmm? From a percentage of his clients' earnings, that's how. And who's his biggest money-maker? You, that's who. And what would happen to his income if you drastically reduced your concert schedule? Now do you see why he didn't want us together? Why he didn't want you depending on me for a major share of your happiness?"

"Let me have my arm back, *cara*. I need to move around. I can't think clearly flat on my back. Okay, say you're right about Arthur's motivation for lying to me. What does my mother get out of breaking us up?"

"Control. Your mother's a very possessive woman where you're concerned. You're her brilliant son, born of her body and raised with every loving care to nurture your incredible gifts and share them with the world. You're her ultimate achievement, the reason she'll be remembered long into the future as the mother of a genius. She also wants to be known, now and in years to come, as the greatest influence in your life— sort of the power behind the throne."

"But she often told me that she wanted me to find the right wife. More than once she speculated on whether my children would inherit my talent."

"Sure she did, Nick. But what do you suppose she meant by the 'right' wife? She was talking about someone who would take second place to her, who would be content with the little time she was allowed with you, who would be perfectly happy to take root at Sea Winds and breed babies while your mother continued to oversee your life and your career. In other words, Nick, my innocent darling, she wanted a proper Old-World Italian wife for you, just like the ones she found for your brothers. They, heaven knows, wouldn't say boo to a goose without Mama's permission."

"They can't help it, *cara*. They were raised very strictly and taught to—"

"Kowtow to their husbands and mother-in-law. I imagine Oriana is just like them, so why didn't you marry her in the first—"

"Marry? Oriana? What are you talking about? Oriana who?"

"Oriana who is the nice, obedient Italian girl you were supposed to marry four years ago, and who is still waiting in the wings while your mother gets rid of me."

"Camille Anders de Conti, I do not understand what the bloody blue blazes you're talking about! I don't know any Oriana. I never knew one. I was never going to marry one."

"Antigori."

"What?"

"Oriana Antigori."

"Anti—Oh, sweet suffering—Somebody's been sending you up. Oriana Antigori is the daughter of my mother's third cousin, and she's all of fourteen years old!"

"Not anymore, she isn't. The marriage was supposed to take place four years ago, just after her eighteenth birthday."

"Nonsense! Aren't you forgetting that we, you and I, were already married four years ago?"

"Your marriage to Oriana had been arranged years before that, according to your mother. Lucianna told me that she and your father had agreed with Oriana's parents on monetary settlements, the date of the wedding, the—"

"Are you serious? Did my mother really tell you that? Why, may I ask, didn't anyone think to inform me of all these marvelous plans?"

"Too distracting. If you'd known too far ahead about this terrific treat, you might not have kept your mind totally on your music."

"Just when was Mother going to—"

"Oh, that fall. You blew all her plans to pieces when you brought me home. She had invited Oriana to visit for a couple of months that autumn, at which time you were supposed to become acquainted. Then at Christmas, so your mother planned, you'd get engaged, and in late spring you'd be married in Italy during your European tour. Very romantic. Great publicity."

"I don't believe—Whatever made Mother think I'd go along with such a—"

"Why not? You always let her plan your life, didn't you? Along with Rossman. Oh, I know you dated some beautiful women over the years, but you'd never shown any signs of being in love with any of them. Why wouldn't Lucianna assume that you'd let her choose a wife for you? And Oriana is apparently just what she was looking for."

"*Is?* Why do you say that? You mentioned something a few minutes ago about her waiting in the wings."

"She is. Nick, why do you think I left last fall?"

"Oh, hell, I don't know, do I? You were sick, I know that, and I guess I—"

"I left because your mother told me that you wanted a divorce, since I couldn't seem to have children, and that you were going to marry Oriana as you'd originally intended before I came along to cast my spell over you. She said that you were so upset about the whole mess that you didn't want to discuss it with me, and that you'd asked her if she would please take care of the details while you were on the Australian tour."

"Cami...*cara*... you *couldn't* have believed that!"

"I didn't...at least, not at first...No, that's wrong...Deep down I know I never really believed it at all, but—You just have no idea the shape I was in then. I was such a mess. It wasn't just losing the baby, although that was an enormous drain both physically and emotionally. Even before that we seemed to be falling apart. I couldn't talk to you...No, I could, but you didn't hear me. You were listening to all the poison your mother was pouring into your ears, and taking her word as gospel. I was so scared when I found out I was pregnant again. After losing the first one, I wanted...wanted you to be with me this time. When I miscarried that first time, you were on the other side of the world, and your mother refused to call you home. I asked for a phone in my room, but she had *her* doctor on the case, and she got him to say I shouldn't be disturbed by calls."

"She told me—"

"Oh, I can imagine she had a perfect excuse—probably putting the blame on me—for not letting you know. Just as she did the second time. Nick, you knew how worried I was—you had to know—yet you couldn't wait to take off for Europe."

"Mother said I was upsetting you by hovering over you. She said you'd settle down once I'd left, and that no woman really wanted a man around while she was—Well, what did I know about women having babies? I believed her. Why wouldn't I, when she'd been through it several times herself? But I did tell her to keep me informed about how you were doing. She seemed uneasy about that new doctor you'd insisted on, and—"

"You bet I insisted on my own doctor. One who wouldn't report back to her and then tell me to follow the regimen she wanted. Oh, there was nothing wrong with it, but there are some options about diet and exercise and stuff, and I wasn't given any choices. Anyhow, I wanted my own doctor, and I was right. He couldn't stop the second miscarriage, but at least *he* took the time and care to find out why I was having so much trouble carrying. I don't suppose your mother bothered to tell you that it's a correctable problem, did she?"

"No! Is it? Why didn't you tell me?"

"When, Nick? By the time you got back from Europe and found out that I'd lost the baby, your mother had you convinced that you should stay away from me. Every time I tried to talk to you, you put me off by insisting I shouldn't dwell on it. Then you'd disappear into the music room or off with someone, and I wouldn't see you for days. You were even sleeping in another part of the house."

"Mother said—"

"Oh, yes, I'll bet she did. What? 'You mustn't disturb poor Cami. She needs her rest. A woman needs to have time to herself to recover from something like this.' Oh, indeed, I can hear her now. Well, let me tell you, my ignorant darling, she lied to you. I needed you. I needed to share *our* loss with you. I needed to tell you that we could have children, that the doctor had discovered that my problem was simply a hormone imbalance that developed in the early stages of pregnancy. Now that he knew about it, he could compensate for it the next time. I needed to have you hold me and—"

"Are you saying that you can really have a baby? That the problem is—But Mother said you'd never be able—"

"Balderdash! Your mother is a—Well, she is. She convinced you to leave for that Australian tour, even though you must have seen what a disaster I was. And once she got you out of the way, she kept hammering at me day after day until I couldn't stand it any longer. Everything just crashed in on me. All the months and years of being left alone in that house, locked behind the walls of Sea Winds, watched and manipulated and criticized until I didn't even feel like myself anymore. I was being smothered to death, and you just kept walking away from me. I had to get out, to get away, to find a place where I could breathe and be me again. There at the end I couldn't even think straight. I was functioning on instinct, and my instinct was telling me to leave. So I left."

"Without telling me. Without letting me know where you were or if you were all right. Did you really think I'd just accept that and forget about you? Oh, Cami."

"I hoped . . . I hoped that you'd find me . . . that you still cared enough to try to find me . . . but months went by, and . . . I'd almost given up when you walked in today. And then nothing went as I'd planned. We were supposed to have this talk *before* we fell into each other's arms. That whole scene up there on the porch wasn't supposed to happen until we'd come to some agreement on—"

"Are you sorry?"

"Are you nuts? It was . . . incredible. It's a wonder we didn't free-fall right off there. What I'm sorry about are those damn splinters. But, Nick, I meant what I said when I agreed to let you sleep here tonight. No more of that until we make some important decisions. It just clouds all the issues. We've done that too often—submerged our problems in a flood of passion. But when we're sated and you've gone again, the problems are still there. What are you doing?"

"Getting dressed."

"But it's the middle of the night. Where are you going?"

"Actually it's after three. No, don't get up. I'll call a cab to take me to the car."

"Nick?"

"It's going to be all right, Cami. I promise. But you've given me a great deal to think about, and there's one thing we unquestionably agree on: I can't think straight when I'm sharing a bed with you. Especially a bed designed for elves."

"Everybody can't afford Olympic-sized beds. When are you—Will you—What—"

"Give me a few days, *cara*. I may take a quick run to Connecticut and possibly New York. Don't look like that, love. I believe everything you've told me, but there are a few things I want to check into myself. I'll call you as soon as I get back. If I promise to behave, will you kiss me good-bye?"

"Mmmm...Nick?...Wait...I want to ask you ...why the hair...all over your face?"

"Disguise. I wanted to be...mmmm, do that...just with you...this summer and to be...able to go...ahhh, witch!...wherever we want without...being recognized. Cami? Didn't you say—"

"Yes, I did, dammit. Why did you start kissing me? No, stop it. Not until—"

"All right, *cara*. I did promise. Oh...the beard. You don't like it?"

"Uh-uh. I can't see what you're thinking. Besides, it makes me itch in some rather tender places. But if you think you need it..."

"We'll see. Let me go now, sweet elf, before I

forget my promise and decide to soothe those tender places. I'll call you in a few days."

"Nick?"

"Yes?"

"I love you."

"I love you, too, *carissima*. Don't ever doubt it again."

"I won't. Good night . . . morning."

"*Ciao*."

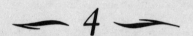

— 4 —

CAMI DIDN'T SEE Nick again until the beginning of
the following week. However, he did change his mind
about calling. Instead of waiting until he returned, he
called her at least once each day, sometimes twice.

The calls were no help in settling Cami's mind.
Nick didn't mention their problems or say one word
about what he was doing. Much to her consternation,
he firmly steered the conversations into neutral waters.
They discussed the weather, the New York traffic,
Cami's latest foray into the world of grubby barns,
and the plans she and Jean had made for participating
in Portland's summer-long celebration of the city's
350th birthday.

Since Nick didn't seem concerned about their immediate future, she also ignored the matter and told
him more than he could possibly have wanted to know
about the history of Portland. When he explained Friday evening that he wouldn't be back for a few more
days, she blandly informed him that she wouldn't have

had time to see him over the weekend anyhow. In answer to his inevitable question, she chuckled and explained that she was attending the world's largest garage sale, then said a quick good-bye and hung up, leaving him to try to figure out what on earth she was talking about.

One way and another, Cami made sure she was out of reach by phone that weekend, and it was a half-anxious, half-angry Nick who strode purposefully into the shop on Monday afternoon. He came to a screeching halt at the sight of Cami standing on an oak icebox, stretching as high as she could to balance a large tin candle-chandelier, which Jean, perched on top of a ladder, was trying to hook over a spike in the center beam.

"Cami, dammit—"

"Oh, Nick, you're just in time," cried Cami, cutting him off in mid-bellow. "We aren't tall enough to get this thing over the hook. I was just about to try putting a chair up here and standing on that to—"

"Spare me, please. I really don't want to hear about it," Nick groaned. "Can you hold that by yourself for a minute, Cami? Come down, Jean, and let me get up there."

Five minutes later Nick stood, hands on hips, surveying the acrobatic duo. "What have you two been doing this time? Crawling around in the cellar?"

Cami and Jean exchanged sheepish looks and burst into laughter. Nick wasn't far off at that, thought Cami, brushing ineffectually at the traces of dust and cobwebs festooning her faded jeans and oldest T-shirt. She glanced at an equally scruffy Jean and wondered if her own hair was as much of a rat's nest as her partner's.

"It was a barn storeroom," explained Jean, trying

to shake her light brown braids free of foreign matter. She grinned up at Nick and added, "We always find the best things in the most inaccessible places."

Cami could tell from the gleam in his eye that he was about to say something outrageous, and she hastily said, "We almost missed the chandelier. It was buried way in a corner under all kinds of junk. We couldn't wait to get it cleaned up and hung, and then Esther had to leave before we could change, and Ronan wasn't around, and—"

"Who's Esther? Who's Ronan?"

"Esther works for us part-time, especially when we both have to be out. Ronan is a . . . friend of Jean's. Her housemate, actually." Cami backed away, edging around an island as she moved toward the storeroom and, more important, the bathroom. "Er . . . Jean, you don't mind if I shower and change first, do you?"

"No, not at all. There's only one or two small boxes to be unloaded." Jean gave Nick's tall figure a laughing once-over, complimented him on his expensive beige linen slacks and burnt-orange silk shirt, and suggested, "Tell you what, Mr. Elegance, since you're not dressed for toting and lifting, you mind the store for a few minutes while I finish the dirty work."

Cami bit her lip and desperately choked back a giggle at Nick's appalled expression. Lucianna would never believe this!

"But what if someone comes in?"

"If it's a man, ask him what he thinks of the Red Sox this season. If it's a woman, charm her!" Cami caroled over her shoulder as she dashed for the shower.

Nick was waiting for her in the storeroom when she emerged from the bathroom half an hour later, her hair still slightly damp from a hasty blow-drying. She doubted if he even noticed it, though, since he was so busy examining the rest of her. The navy cotton sundress was one of her favorites, with the field of daisies and devil's paintbrush silk-screened around the bottom half of the gathered skirt. Her high-heeled white sandals brought the top of her head up to his chin. *His chin!*

"You shaved!" she squealed.

"I wondered when you were going to notice," Nick drawled, wrapping both hands around her small waist and lifting her to eye level. "I also wondered when you were going to kiss me hello."

Cami slid her arms around his neck and met his laughing look with a smile of her own. "I didn't want to get smudges on all that elegance." She brushed a light kiss across his lips and murmured throatily, "Hello, big boy."

Nick shook his head, laughing, and set her back on her feet. "That's an atrocious Mae West. You just haven't got enough . . . ah . . . chest to do it right. Not that I'm complaining, love. You're perfect for me exactly as you are. Now, let's try that hello kiss again, hmmm?"

"I can't believe I didn't notice that you'd shaved."

"What else could I do? After all, those tender places . . ."

Cami leaned back in her chair and took another sip of her wine. "This isn't the time to discuss my tender spots." She looked around the familiar dining room of Harbor House, commenting, "I take it you like this place."

"Not bad. The food is good, the service doesn't interfere with conversation, and it's reasonably quiet."

"You're getting pretty feisty, aren't you?"

"Feisty?"

"Independent, then." Cami grinned at him and raised a mocking eyebrow. "No Gavin—again. You made the reservations yourself—again. Are you driving yourself again?"

"No. Gavin dropped me off. He'll pick us up later and drive us down to the Cape." Nick gave her his most charming smile.

"Oh, no, you don't. I told you—"

He leaned across the table and captured her waving hand. "Calm down, *cara*. I really do want you to see the Cattons' place."

"Why? Nick, I told you I can't stay way down there. It's too far to commute."

"Yes, well, there are a number of things we have to discuss," Nick said, leaning back to let the waiter serve large main-course salads heaped with lobster and king-crab meat.

"That sounds a trifle ominous," she murmured, most of her attention fixed on the mouth-watering salad. She flashed a quick look at her obstinate husband and caught the watchfulness in his expression. He was up to something. "Can this discussion wait until later?" she asked hopefully. "I'd like to enjoy this scrumptious-looking concoction."

"All right. We'll talk later," he agreed in an indulgent tone that had Cami gritting her teeth.

After a few minutes of his coaxing and teasing, she finally ungritted them, and she kept him laughing throughout dinner with her description of that gigantic sale, a "Celebration 350" event sponsored by a Portland TV station. Nick's experiences in the capitals of the world had included neither garage sales nor the fine points of bargaining. He was fascinated at Cami's and Jean's determination in acquiring a great many potentially valuable somethings for next to nothing.

"What on earth are green-handled kitchen tools,

and what's so great about buying them for a dime apiece?"

"I'll show you some the next time you're in the shop," she said, laughing at his bewilderment. "And what's so great about a dime apiece is that most of them sell for several dollars each. They're starting to be collected now, so we sell them as fast as we find them."

Cami sobered abruptly and became very intent on fixing her coffee just so. It's time, she thought, and she crossed her fingers under the edge of the table. *Please, Nick, make this a real discussion, not your usual series of pronouncements.*

"Okay, Nick, let's have it," she said, a faint touch of resignation mixed with the hopeful tone of her voice. "What did you find out in Connecticut, and what do you want to discuss?"

"Connecticut. You mean did I confront my mother, don't you?" he specified.

He stared pensively out the window, his eyes following the riding lights of a large boat moving across the harbor, while he debated how much to tell Cami. The discussions with his mother and the other members of his family had been difficult and painfully disillusioning, full of accusations, tears, recriminations, and, ultimately, apologies. His confrontation with Arthur Rossman had also been distressing.

For the first time in his life Nick was forced to face the reality of human fallibility—both his own and that of the people who had always been closest to him. He had blindly trusted his mother, his family, and his manager, believing that they had his best interests at heart. After all, hadn't they all, from as far back as he could remember, been dedicated to nurturing and developing his talent to its fullest potential? The de Conti family's great wealth, by itself, would have cushioned him from the harsher realities of life, but his supporters had gone beyond that in their desire to spare him even the smallest distractions. He had been totally free to live in and with his music. He hadn't had to think about anything else. Until Cami.

He'd seen her, loved her, and decided he needed her in his life. He had made the necessary adjustments in his routine and lifestyle to provide a special place for her. Had she been right that time she'd screamed at him that he was treating her like a doll, something he could take out and amuse himself with when he was in the mood and then put away until he wanted it again?

He'd believed he was doing the right thing in leaving her safe and protected at *I Venti di Mare* while he traveled. Everyone had agreed she'd be much happier with the family to amuse her and coddle her than she would be spending hours alone in strange places. Everyone—but Cami. She'd tried to tell him, but he'd been deaf to her pleas and arguments. His mother had assured him that everything was going reasonably well, despite some minor problems of adjustment on Cami's part. Of course he'd believed her assessment that Cami was high-strung, moody, and argumentative; she was that way whenever he was home, and he'd naturally agreed with his mother that Cami would be better off in the peaceful environment of the estate.

Lord, how could he have been so blind and self-centered, willfully ignoring anything that interfered with his concentration on his music and his career? He still found it almost impossible to believe the truth he had forced from his dismayed family and his nervous manager over the past few days. It would be a while yet before he could completely forgive them, but at least there would be no more of these upsets.

He had made his terms quite clear. From now on Cami should be much happier.

"Nick? Hey, where have you gone?"

"Sorry, my anxious lady," he said, taking her hand in a warm clasp. "Of course you want to know our plans."

Our?

"I had long talks with Mother and the rest of the family, as well as with Arthur. They admitted that much of what you told me was true."

Oh? How much?

"Try to understand, *cara*," Nick pleaded. "It was very difficult for me to hear them all confess that they had lied, not once but many times. They feel terrible about it."

Mostly at being caught out, I'll bet.

"They truly believed that they were acting in my best interests, that you had somehow trapped me into marrying you for money and advantage, and that they were saving me from my own folly by driving you away."

And if you believe that, let me tell you about Peter Pan!

"Cami?"

"Go on, Nick. I'm listening."

He eyed her deliberately impassive expression, wishing he knew what was going on in her head, but then continued, "I'm sure I've convinced them that they were totally wrong. Everyone has promised that things will be much better in the future. They're ready to accept you completely as my wife, the most important person in my life."

Your mother will never accept that, no matter what she promises.

"Cami? Do you understand? They're all eager to make amends. Things will be so much better now. You'll see."

"What am I going to see, Nick? Just what are you expecting me to do?"

He saw the wariness in her eyes and ached for the pain he had caused her through his neglect and misjudgment. How long, he wondered, would it be before she trusted him again? He must make that his first priority this summer.

"I think you'll agree that I've given careful thought to our plans."

There's that "our" again.

"We need to spend time together to build that closeness you were talking about. Just the two of us. Nobody else—but Gavin, of course."

Terrific.

"The fact that you've got this Esther already working part-time solves one problem. I was going to suggest that you hire such a person so you could cut down your hours. I understand, *cara,* why you feel you can't abandon Jean completely right at the start of your busiest season, and I'm perfectly willing for you to work three or four days a week for a few hours."

Oh, are you now!

"We can put your furniture in storage or send it home, and you can move down to the Cattons' with me. The commuting is no problem. Gavin has assured me that he'll be happy to chauffeur you."

In my truck?

"We'll have three months by ourselves, and I see no reason, if both of us are determined, that we can't recapture the marvelous rapport we had in the beginning."

Cami held up a restraining hand and quirked her right eyebrow. "I get the picture, Nick. But what happens at the end of the summer?"

"By then you and Jean will have found someone to buy out your share of the shop, and we'll go home. "

"Home? Just what home is that, my devious lord?"

asked Cami with a sinking feeling that she knew all
too well what the answer would be.

Nick shifted in his chair with uncharacteristic ner-
vousness. He knew this was going to be the tricky
part.

"I Venti di Mare, of course. It's the only home we
have." He spoke a little faster and louder so she couldn't
easily interrupt. "It will be different, *cara.* I promise.
We'll have our own house. If you don't like the ones
available, we'll build a new one just the way you want
it. You'll have your own car, and you can come and
go as you please. You can even work part-time if you
want to keep busy. No one will interfere with us. And
we'll plan the next baby more carefully. Maybe wait
a year or so, and in the meantime you can come with
me on a couple of tours. It will be—"

"No."

"No?"

"No."

"But, Cami, *carissima,* I don't understand. It's
what you said you wanted, isn't it? Have I forgotten
something?"

Cami sighed, feeling a mixture of exasperation and
fading anger. She knew it was futile to wind herself
up over his authoritarian attitude. It was instinctive
rather than consciously assumed; the belief in the natural superiority of the male had been inculcated in
him, through both training and example, from the time
he could walk. She had even wondered sometimes if
it was hereditary.

How many hours had she sat listening to one or
another of the family—usually Lucianna—discourse
on the history of the de Contis? For a while it had
been fascinating. Titled, wealthy, and for centuries
politically active in the convoluted power games of
the ruling Italian families, the de Contis had been

diligent in recording the history of the generations and their times. When Pietro narrowly escaped Napoleon's secret police and fled to safety in the New World with his wife and two young sons, he renounced his title in favor of his younger brother, but, with practical forethought, took along a generous share of the family's transportable wealth. With that and a shrewd eye for the unlimited investment opportunities in a new country on the verge of tremendous expansion, Pietro had founded the de Contis' American financial empire.

He and his equally aristocratic wife had also established a tradition when they chose their sons' wives from the Italian nobility. This practice continued through the generations, at least in the case of the eldest son, thus ensuring that Pietro's descendants were raised with the culture and philosophy of the European aristocracy—particularly with regard to the so-called natural roles of male and female.

Nick was not the first de Conti to take a non-Italian wife. Occasionally over the years a younger son had chosen a wife from a country other than Italy—even an American with a strong European heritage—but always they were women who understood their "proper place" in the family. Nick was, however, the first de Conti to bring home an American wife whose heritage was three hundred years of New England independence spiced with thirty years of California free-style living. Oil and water were a perfect blend compared to Nick and Cami's divergent views on women, their place in the natural order of things, or even just what that natural order was.

Cami studied Nick's perplexed expression. *Nodcock! He really hasn't a clue. He thinks he's overlooked one of my "terms" for coming back to him. Is he really seeing this as some kind of battle? Does he*

*honestly believe I was setting my terms of surrender
in that midnight discussion? He obviously missed one
of the main points, since he's still doing his chauvinist
number. Heigh-ho, my domineering Dominic, if you
want a battle, I'll damn well give you a war! Hang
on to your arpeggios, sweetie; you're about to get
blasted out of your curricle right into the space age!*

Giving Nick her best Cheshire-cat smile, Cami said
dulcetly, "You've forgotten several things, dear heart,
not least of which is the art of discussion."

Nick tensed. He'd seen that smile in the past, just
before his darling did or said something utterly outrageous.

"I thought we discussed all of this the other night,"
he suggested cautiously. "You know, just after we—"

"I know exactly when," Cami interjected hastily.
"However, that was an examination—actually, it was
more of an explanation—of past history. I don't recall
that we *discussed* anything about where we go from
here. I'm sure I'd remember if I'd been consulted
about my future plans, immediate or otherwise."

Nick opted for amusement. She did it so well: the
half-cocked eyebrow, the slight tilt of her head, just
the faintest hint of sardonic inquiry. There was no
point in becoming upset over her contrariness. She
didn't really mean it; she was simply trying to send
him up. But tonight he wasn't in the mood for games.
He wanted to get her home and into that big bed—
thank heaven the Cattons had decent-sized beds!—
and take up where they'd left off the other night up
in her crazy tower. It was time to apply a firm but
gentle hand.

"We really should be on our way, *cara*. Gavin will
be here with the car in a few minutes." Nick stood
and waited for Cami to join him. "I'm sure we're
basically in agreement, and we can iron out any little

problems during the ride home."

Cami restrained her strong desire to crown him with a potted palm. The main dining room of Harbor House was not the place to assault and batter her blockhead of a husband.

"There's no need to hurry, Cami. Gavin will wait." Nick lengthened his stride to keep up with her rapid pace and barely had time to open the heavy outer door before she was through it and moving swiftly toward Moulton Street.

"Cami! Where are you going?" He caught her arm and swung her around, glaring down at her as he easily prevented her escape. "What's the matter? Didn't you hear me say Gavin was picking us up?"

"Not me, he isn't," she snapped, her eyes flashing with temper. "I told you before that I wasn't going to the Cattons' house. You simply don't listen, Nick."

"But you don't have to drive in in the morning. Gavin will—"

"Nick!" Cami yelled at the top of her lungs, effectively stopping all pedestrians within a hundred feet. "Read my lips: I . . . am . . . not . . . going . . . home . . . with . . . you. Got it?"

His "Nonsense!" was only a few decibels below a full bellow. "Of course you're going—"

"Is this guy botherin' you, ma'am? Won't be no trouble to send 'im on his way."

Cami turned startled eyes to the large barrel-chested man who had materialized beside them. His grizzled hair and well-worn face indicated middle age, but the muscles straining the seams of his plaid shirt and faded chinos spoke of a physical fitness that could take on two or three Nicks. She saw nothing but fatherly concern in the pale blue eyes fixed inquiringly on her face. However, his expression changed drastically as he turned to scowl warningly at Nick.

"Er . . . thank you very much, but that won't be necessary," Cami said, smiling warmly at her erstwhile rescuer. From the corner of her eye, she noted that an interested crowd had gathered, and she realized she had better defuse the situation in a hurry. "It's nothing I can't handle. Really. But I do appreciate your concern."

"Well . . . if you're sure, ma'am," he growled doubtfully, looking from her petite figure to Nick's impressive build. His eyes dropped to Nick's hands, which were still wrapped around Cami's upper arms. "I'd feel a sight better, though," he said judiciously, "if you'd just let loose of the little lady, mister. Don't see the need to be grabbin' at 'er and scarin' 'er half to death."

Cami glanced up at Nick and choked back a peal of laughter. His expression was a fascinating mixture of affronted dignity and astonishment. She knew that he could never, in his wildest nightmares, have envisioned himself in the middle of a scene like this. He stiffened, and as his head went back and he looked scathingly down his nose at her champion, she could almost see thirty-odd generations of proudly disdainful de Contis ranging themselves behind him.

"I can assure you, *signore,*" Nick began in a tone that once caused serfs to revolt, "that there is—"

His comment was cut off and all heads turned as a maroon Rolls-Royce swerved to the curb with a discreet squeal of brakes. It had barely stopped before a burly man in a gray chauffeur's uniform erupted from the driver's door and hastened to Nick's side.

"Is there a problem, Mr. Dominic?" he asked in a beautifully modulated English accent.

"Gavin," groaned Cami, taking in the familiar placid expression, the alert brown eyes, and the rugged physique of Nick's valet/chauffeur/bodyguard. This was all she needed now—Gavin and her hero getting into a brawl.

"Now just a minute," growled her hero. "You two ain't gonna be gangin' up—"

"Who is this person, sir? Shall I—"

"He's an interfering busybody, Gavin, and you can—Ooowww..."

Cami shifted her weight more firmly onto the heel she'd planted on Nick's instep, muttering at Nick and Gavin, "Shut up, you idiots, before you start a riot. Can't you see that the crowd isn't at all pleased about you two big bullies picking on fragile little me? Now you just go get in the car while I thank the nice people."

"Camille—"

"Go now, Nick. You, too, Gavin. Move it, guys, before that sweet man decides to punch you out."

Cami flashed a placating smile at the sweet man as she moved between Nick and Gavin and, planting a hand firmly in the middle of each broad back, gave them a hearty shove in the direction of the Rolls. She turned back to her new friend and held out her hand.

"I want to thank you so much for offering your assistance. In this case, as you can see, it wasn't needed. We were just having a slight marital disagreement." She grinned at him conspiratorially and winked at the now-amused bystanders. A ripple of laughter went through the crowd as she continued, "I'm new to Portland, and I can't tell you how safe it makes me feel to know that people here aren't afraid to step in and help when they think it's necessary." Oh, was she ever slathering it on! "You've all been so kind. I do appreciate it. Good night, now."

To a chorus of rather self-conscious good nights, Cami strode briskly to the car. She could just hear the almost inaudible purr of the well-tuned engine, and she knew that Gavin, sitting ramrod-straight behind the wheel, was ready to move as soon as she joined Nick in the back seat. He had conveniently left the rear door open for her. She gave it a hefty slam as she marched past on her way around to the driver's door.

"Move over, Gavin," she snapped as she opened the door. "I'm driving."

"But, Mrs. Dominic," he protested, using the formal address she hadn't heard in months, "you can't—"

"Move it, Gavin, or I'll call my tame gorilla back. I'm not in the best of moods, and—" She stopped as the glass partition behind the front seat lowered and Nick leaned forward, his eyes dark with anger. Before he could speak, she matched him glare for glare and growled, "Don't you dare say another word, Dominic de Conti. I don't trust you an inch. *I'm* driving this car to my parking lot. That way I'll know where I'm going and won't find myself halfway to Cape Elizabeth after telling you I don't want to go there."

By the time she had to pause for breath, Nick had given in and signaled Gavin to slide over. He settled back in his seat, watching his small wife smoothly wheel the big car through the streets of the Old Port, while he seethed with frustration and temper.

I don't believe any of this happened. My Lord, what if there'd been a reporter in that crowd! Dominic de Conti and wife in a common street brawl. Marvelous. Just wait until I get her alone, preferably in a soundproof room where we can yell all we want to without any blasted busybodies butting in.

Cami had only half her attention on the mechanics of the short drive, while the other half of her mind was busily sorting through her options. She did spare a quick glance for Gavin. He didn't look at all pleased, she decided, but then he'd never been overly fond of her from the beginning.

She'd long ago concluded that Gavin was more than a little jealous of her place in her husband's life. Some ten years older than Nick and intensely loyal, Gavin had been with him since Nick was sixteen and starting his first concert tour. In the ensuing seventeen years, Gavin had been at Nick's side every day, except for the rare occasions when he traveled ahead by a day or two to make special arrangements—and that one vacation he'd taken five years ago. Until Cami came along, Gavin had been closer to Nick than anyone else. She suspected that he blamed himself for leaving Nick alone that summer, bored and easy prey for the first attractive girl who caught his eye.

Tough tacos, Gavin, but if we get back together, you're just going to have to change your ways. No more of that "Mr. Dominic is otherwise engaged, madam" nonsense every time I want to talk to Nick. No more disapproving sniffs when you find our clothes scattered around the bedroom in the morning. And absolutely no more discreet interruptions every damn time we manage to find some privacy.

Cami braked to a smooth stop beside her truck and quickly slid out of the car. Nick moved just as quickly to block her way, slamming the car door behind him.

"Slow down, Cami. You're not going anywhere until we've discussed—"

"Ah, *discussion*," she said thoughtfully, a smile on her lips. "I've been thinking about that. Tomorrow is impossible. I'm going to be up to my ears all day, and it's one of my nights to close at nine. Sooo...it will have to be Wednesday. Let's see, I need time to go home and change...Seven-thirty should be about right...Yes, Nick, you can pick me up at my place at seven-thirty. Dinner and dancing would be nice. It's been a long time since we went dancing."

"Dancing?" Nick felt as if he'd fallen into the middle of someone else's conversation. "Cami, I want to talk to you. We've got to decide——"

"Yes, yes, I know, but first things first," she admonished. "That's been the problem all along, I think. We never did take time to get acquainted properly, to really find out where each of us was coming from. It was whiz, whoosh, and zip, we were married. I've decided that what we need is to go back to the beginning, to the basics, and start over again. We can date for a while——there's no hurry, since you've got the whole summer off——and then you can court me properly, and then——"

"Date you? Court you?" Nick's eyes fastened on her lips. Yes, she'd really said that. "What on earth are you babbling about? Cami, in case it's escaped your notice, we've been married for almost five years. I'll be damned if I'll go back to hand-holding and chaste kisses when I want you——"

"Hmmm, I know what you want," she said absently, her eyes fixed in an unfocused stare over his shoulder.

"Well, then?"

She cocked her head and gave him a considering look. "You know, Nick, I can't recall one single chaste kiss. They were all hot, passionate, steamy, sensual, and guaranteed to melt my knees. I'll bet you don't even know *how* to kiss chastely."

Nick stared at her in what was rapidly becoming a permanent state of bewilderment. "How did we get into this? Who wants to kiss chastely? Especially your wife . . . my wife . . . you. I don't want to kiss you chastely," he said plaintively. "I want to melt your knees."

"Well, you can't. I mean you *can* . . . at least, you did the other night . . . but you can't do it again until I say so because it muddies up the waters and——"

"Stop!" Nick heaved a long sigh of pure exasperation and wondered when his darling, reasonably intelligent wife had become so capricious. "Cami, you're beginning to sound like one of those flighty females in those Regencies of yours. You aren't making the least bit of sense. All I can get out of this is that you want to date, have a courtship with chaste kisses, knee-melting is out, and pure water is in."

"You got it!" she cried with an admiring smile.

"Terrific. Now tell me, simply, just what it is I've got."

Cami clutched her hair with both hands and groaned. This was ridiculous. She couldn't really blame Nick for being confused. She knew she wasn't explaining anything clearly, but she hadn't really expected to get into this in the middle of a parking lot, with Gavin sitting nearby, after a very trying evening. She'd planned to sit down with him and lay it all out logically and concisely.

Drawing a deep, calming breath, she met Nick's quizzical gaze with what she hoped was a look of firm purpose.

"I want to put our marriage back together, Nick, and I know you want the same thing. What we seem to disagree on is how to do it. I'll admit there's a lot of appeal in the thought of spending most of the summer together, making love, relaxing in the sun, and enjoying ourselves. But then what? Go back to Sea Winds? Back behind those walls that close out the rest of the world? Back to the intrusive, smothering, inescapable presence of your family?"

"I told you that they—"

"No, Nick, they won't stand back and not interfere. I don't care what they promised you." She paused before she hit him between the eyes with her one nonnegotiable decision. Everything else was open for debate, but not this. "Nick, listen to me. I've had months to think about this, and one thing is very clear. We can't survive as husband and wife and make a real marriage as long as we live at Sea Winds. Even if we straighten out all our other problems, it will be for nothing if we go back there to live."

Nick regarded her intently for a long moment. "Are you saying that you won't return to Sea Winds under any circumstances? Even if I can guarantee that things will be very different this time?"

"Yes, Nick, that's what I'm saying," she replied softly, simultaneously fighting down the fear that he wouldn't accept this and struggling to hold on to her resolution. "I know this is something you need time to think about. While you're doing that, let's work on some of the other problems, the biggest of which—"

"Cami—"

". . . is communication. I'm going to teach you the art of discussion if it kills both of us."

"And what I want to discuss right now—"

"Not now, Nick. Wednesday evening. We've got a date, remember? Seven-thirty at my place," she called as she scrambled into her truck.

"Cami!"

Her only acknowledgment was a wave as she pulled out of the parking lot. Nick stood with his feet spread and his fists planted on his hips, watching in frustration as she sped away down Harborside Lane.

"You may have had the last word this time, you contrary little witch, but we'll see how you like it when I play this game your way. Chaste kisses! I'll give you chaste kisses that'll straighten your hair!"

"Mr. Dominic? Did you say something?"

"Nothing you'd be interested in, Gavin. Let's go. I've got a problem to solve."

"Anything I can help you with?"

"Not unless you know how to handle hot pot roast without getting burned." Seeing Gavin's puzzled expression, Nick chuckled and added, "Don't worry about it. There's more than one way to goose a cook—or pot a roast."

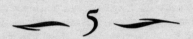

5

"MY POOR FEET may never be the same," Jean groaned, collapsing onto the blue and white webbing of the aluminum lounger and gently wiggling her bare toes. "Where did all those people come from?"

"Who'd have expected a crowd like that on a Monday?" Cami leaned back in a matching lawn chair and propped her bare feet on the bottom of the lounger. "As near as I could make out, half of them were the regular tourist influx, and the rest were locals who didn't want to miss out on any of the Celebration 350 events. At least they had one thing in common: They all wanted to spend money."

Cami shook her hair back, enjoying the touch of the cool evening breeze coming off Casco Bay. She took a sip of iced tea and watched the small boats cruising just offshore.

"It's so peaceful up here," Jean murmured. "I wish I'd seen it first."

"I have to admit that this porch more than makes up for that weird kitchen."

"And that equally weird bathroom. Has Nick seen that?"

"Oh, yes," said Cami with a gurgle of laughter. "He's cracked his head twice and had several untranslatable things to say about people who get too cute for words when renovating old houses."

"You must admit that it's a few points beyond original to turn a landing and part of a double staircase into a bathroom." Jean smiled reminiscing. "I'll never forget the first time I saw it. You, you devious twit, didn't even warn me. I opened that door thinking it was a closet and almost fell down the steps."

"And then you yelled something about it being a strange place for a staircase," Cami chimed in.

"And you called back that it wasn't a staircase, it was the bathroom. I thought you were putting me on."

"So did Nick," Cami gasped between giggles. "Oh, you should have seen his face when he asked me where he could wash up, and I told him to go down four steps to find the sink, then to the end of the room and up three steps on the left to the john, and down two steps on the right to the shower. He stared at me as if I'd grown a second head. I got laughing so hard I forgot to tell him about that odd ceiling angle over the toilet. Let me tell you, he knows some Italian that never gets near a phrase book."

"I can believe it," Jean said dryly. "And speaking of Nick's temper, how is your great experiment going? It's been, what, two weeks now? Don't tell me you've actually managed to keep his lusty libido on ice all this time."

"I wouldn't exactly call our relationship icy," Cami said ruefully. "It's more like an eager simmer. He's taking this whole thing as a challenge, you know. I never should have mentioned chaste kisses," she moaned.

Jean's grin was far from sympathetic. "Given the nature of the beast, that was rather stupid. What's he doing?"

"Kissing me chastely on the forehead while his damn Roman hands wander all over me. I swear he's got at least six of them. I no sooner pluck one off me than three more land on my prime erogenous zones. Stop laughing, you traitor; it's not funny. He's got me walking around with my nipples in a permanent pucker."

Jean's infectious laughter finally set Cami off, and, much to Nick's amusement, neither of them heard his footsteps coming up the turret stairs. He leaned against the doorjamb and watched the two women rocking with laughter and wiping away tears of mirth. Since he'd missed the conversation that had inspired such hilarity, his appreciative grin was due mostly to the sight of a great deal of bare skin, attractively revealed by the skimpy shorts and brief camisole top his darling was wearing. When the giggling finally faded to gasps, he drawled, "It's the noonday sun that's supposed to send everyone mad. Leave it to you two to be crazed by the setting sun."

"Nick!" wheezed Cami, still trying to get her breath back. "You're early."

Jean couldn't manage more than a weak smile and a wave as Nick dropped into the chair nearest Cami.

"Not early enough, it seems," he commented, looking from one limp figure to the other. He picked up Cami's iced tea and took a couple of long swallows. "What set you two off? If I'd known you were perched up here telling raunchy stories, I'd have—"

"Nick!" Cami yelped, her mouth dropping open and a slow tide of red creeping up her neck as she remembered just what she'd said to Jean.

Nick noted both the blush and the guilty look and

gave his wife a knowing smile as he murmured provocatively, "Just what do you girls talk about when no men are around?"

"Er...did you get a chance to see the *State of Maine?*" Cami asked hastily, referring to the Maine Maritime Academy's training ship. The Tall Ship was docked at the harbor and open for tours for three days as part of Celebration 350.

"Not yet," he answered, magnanimously deciding to allow the switch of subject. "You two look as if you're settled in here for the evening. Change of plans?"

"Uh-uh. You're early," Cami reminded him.

"And Ronan will probably be late," said Jean.

"So we figured on another half-hour before we had to dress," ended Cami.

"Fine by me," sighed Nick, stretching his long legs out and relaxing in his chair. "This is the coolest spot I've been in today."

Their talk was desultory as they attempted to recover from the nearly record-breaking temperature of the late June day. Cami poured more iced tea into Jean's glass and then replenished the one she and Nick were sharing. For a moment she thought about running downstairs to get him his own glass, but she immediately gave up the idea when she considered the return trip.

What would he do, she wondered, if she suggested that he go get a glass for himself? She tried to picture the possible expressions on his face: incomprehension? confusion? surprise? annoyance? No, not annoyance. He was never deliberately thoughtless. It wasn't his fault that he'd been brought up to expect everything to be done for him. Lucianna had taught him from the beginning to ask for anything he wanted, and had instilled the idea that fetching and carrying were the responsibilities of servants and hotel employees.

Gavin had taken over where Lucianna left off, picking up after Nick, anticipating his wishes, doing a hundred and one things for him that other people did for themselves, and practically forbidding him to do so much as dial a telephone by himself. It was amazing, thought Cami with a silent burst of laughter, that Gavin never tried to undress her and pop her into bed, all ready and waiting for Nick's pleasure—which led to another thought...

Nick and Jean stared uncomprehendingly as Cami suddenly doubled over in a paroxysm of laughter.

"Oh...oh...I can't...stand it," she gasped, their expressions bringing on a fresh burst of mirth.

"What in the world is so funny?" asked a bewildered Jean.

"If it's that good, elf, share it."

She wiped the tears from her cheeks, shaking her head at their continued questions. They'd think she'd popped her chimney pot if she tried to explain the vivid technicolor fantasy that had filled her mind. How could she describe her vision of Nick, dressed in rich brocaded robes and lolling on a huge silk-draped divan, watching Gavin, in formal butler's attire, walk along a row of nubile maidens, efficiently removing their gossamer costumes with all the interest and enthusiasm of a man shucking ears of corn, while he intoned in an impeccable English accent: "Be quick and agile. The master must not exert himself. Be unobtrusive. The master must not be distracted from his mind-music. Be imaginative. Above all, the master must be pleasured."

The replay of her scenario brought on a fresh bout of laughter, and Jean and Nick chorused another demand to "Tell us what's so damn funny!"

"C–can't . . . im–impossible . . . You h–had to b–be there," Cami stammered between fits of giggles.

"Whatever she's on, I'll take some," announced a deep voice from the doorway.

"Hi, darling, you're early," said Jean, shifting her legs to make room for the colorfully attired man strolling toward her.

His response—"From the maestro's look of frustration, I'd say I arrived in the nick of time"—brought forth groans from Jean and Nick and another gurgle of laughter from Cami.

"Please, Ronan," Nick begged, "don't start her off again."

Cami limited herself to a wave as Ronan gingerly sat down by Jean's legs. Involved for the moment in regaining her composure, Cami let the bantering of the other three wash over her. Finally, feeling in control again, she shifted her gaze to Ronan and made an appreciative examination of his version of casual attire for a warm summer evening.

It fell somewhere between eccentric and mind-boggling. Of course there were places—Provincetown, Fire Island, and southern California, for example— where no one would bat an eye at sandals, billowy wide-legged pants of thin black satin glittering with interwoven silver threads, a three-inch belt of bargello needlepoint in a hot pink, orange, and yellow abstract design, a buttonless silver tissue shirt with wide, scalloped-edged elbow-length sleeves, and, as a crowning touch, a jaunty orange Robin Hood cap with yellow and pink plumes. Even in Portland, Maine, Cami knew, this costume—along with some of Ronan's other sartorial originalities—might not cause more than a curious look and a chuckle if worn by a young, slim, obviously artistically inclined male. However, when such an outfit was draped over thirty-six-year-old

Ronan's 210 pounds of bulging muscles and heavy bones, which were impressively arrayed on a six-foot-plus, broad-shouldered, deep-chested frame, the effect was nothing short of stupendous.

Cami listened with interest to the debate he and Nick were having on private versus public ownership of great artworks. The easy friendship that had sprung up between the two men was still a source of amused conjecture between Cami and Jean. No two men could have been more dissimilar than wealthy, sophisticated, internationally famous Nick, with his conservatively elegant taste, and tough, outspoken, half-Gypsy Ronan, whose fine arts degree had been earned by alternating months as a heavy-construction worker with semesters at college. Once he had discovered the direction of his creative talents and interests, Ronan had worked for two more years, saving every possible cent, so he could serve a full-time apprenticeship and then set himself up as a goldsmith.

Now, five years later, he was beginning to receive recognition, not only for his unique jewelry, but also for the small, exquisitely crafted bibelots he created, à la Fabergé, on commission for discriminating collectors of unusual art forms. Even after watching him work, Cami still found it hard to believe that those huge, callused hands could perform such delicate tasks.

"Hey-yo, Cami, we'd better get changed if we're going to make it for the first round," said Jean, glancing at her watch. She gave Ronan's costume a significant look and said, laughing, "We don't want to be conspicuous by arriving late."

"Heaven forbid," Cami agreed, coming to her feet. She leaned over the back of Nick's chair and whispered loudly, "And you worry about being recognized. No one's even going to *see* you with Ronan along."

"One good turn deserves another," said Nick cryptically as he winked at the other man.

"Do you know what that was all about?" Jean called a few minutes later as she stripped off her shorts and top in Cami's bedroom.

Cami's answer was a muffled "Nope" as she rooted around in the far end of the huge walk-in closet-cum-dressing room that took up most of the second floor of the ell connecting the octagonal bay to the main house. She eventually emerged dangling a pair of mint-green canvas sling-backs.

"I have an idea they're cooking up something," she said, dropping her shoes and swinging Jean around to fasten the small buttons at the neck of her pale pink halter-top dress. "I just haven't figured out what yet. Did you know this dress has absolutely no back above the waist?"

"And you get one guess as to who picked it out," said Jean ruefully. "The things I wear for that man. My mother would turn puce if she saw this. Just look at the neckline."

"Want to borrow a pin?"

"Want to know what the man-mountain said when I suggested wearing one?"

"Never mind," said Cami, chuckling. "I can imagine. It looks good on you, though. I'm just surprised the skirt isn't skintight with a slit all the way to Nirvana."

"Impossible. I'm informed my tush is not made for tight skirts."

"Well, considering that neckline, it's a good thing your superstructure is made for filling out—"

"Forget it," Jean said hastily. "What are you wearing besides those shoes? Five more minutes and we'll be hearing the thud of big feet on the stairs. It's a good thing we showered earlier." She raised her voice as Cami retreated to the dressing room. "I love this bedroom, but don't you feel as if you're living in a goldfish bowl?"

One of the eight walls in the large octagonal room was taken up by the doorway to the hall, while each of the other seven walls contained a wide seven-foot-high window. Jean wandered from window to window, skirting the bed, which was, of necessity, placed in the middle of the room, and dodging the walnut bedside stands, a small cameo-back boudoir chair, and an oblong marble-topped lamp table.

"Where did I put—Oh, there they are," Cami exclaimed, skipping into the room and scooping up her shoes. She sat on the edge of the bed to put them on. "You don't think we'll get a thunderstorm, do you? I'd hate to close the windows now that there's such a lovely breeze."

"Doesn't look it," Jean answered absently. "You never really said how you were making out with Nick's re-education. Have you got him discussing anything important yet? I like that dress. Can he understand how you feel about Sea Winds?"

"I think we're making some progress," Cami said.

She stood up and adjusted the softly flared knee-length skirt of her cocoa-brown dress. Broad bands of mint-green, yellow, and white bordered the skirt, while narrower matching bands trimmed the wide boat neckline and flaring elbow-length sleeves. A pair of small gold conical shells dangling from her ears and a similar shell suspended from a delicate gold bracelet completed her costume.

"He's at least asking questions and listening to the answers," Cami continued, "and he's starting to discuss ideas instead of simply making pronouncements. Is your hair going to stay in that twist, or do you want another couple of pins?"

"I don't think there's room for any more," Jean answered, carefully patting the back of her head. "It'd better stay in. If it falls down, my earrings won't show."

"Ah, Ronan's been at it again, I see," Cami murmured as she moved closer to examine the lovely cloisonné ovals swinging from Jean's ears. "Hark! I hear the clump of big feet. Are we ready?"

"Ayuh," said Jean, using the familiar Maine term for *yes, maybe, I guess so, okay,* and *perhaps.* When ending with a rising inflection, it could express doubt, disbelief, amazement, or curiosity. Cami was still trying to master its many inflections and uses.

"Are you having a good time?" asked Cami, leaning close to Nick so he could hear her above the noise of the jazz band and the happy crowd filling the Brigantine's back dining room.

"Yes. Are you surprised?" Nick grinned down into her hazel eyes, which were sparkling with excitement and three glasses of wine.

"Yes. No. Well, you have to admit it's not like those teddibly posh do's you're used to," mocked Cami in a garbled English accent.

"No, it's not. Maybe that's why I'm enjoying it so much," he countered.

"Do you expect me to believe you prefer a good jazz band to string quartets and opera stars?"

"For a party like this? Of course." Nick held her eyes with his intent, questioning look. "After all these years, do you see me as a snob, Cami? Good music is good music, just as nice people are nice people. That's an exceptionally good jazz band, and these Old Port compatriots of your have been very warm and friendly to me. These are, on the whole, creative people, and almost all creative people have some basics in common. Why shouldn't I like and understand them?"

Cami stared back at him, saw the truth in his eyes, and grimaced ruefully. "I'm sorry. It was a stupid remark. Sometimes, I'm afraid, I find it hard to separate you from your family."

"What's that supposed to mean?" he asked.

"Think about it a minute." Cami turned to face him more fully, the happy throng around them temporarily forgotten. "We've been married almost five years. For the first two months we avoided other people because we wanted to be alone. After that, we were always, *always,* with your family whenever you were home between tours. We never seemed to go anywhere by ourselves. We did all our socializing with people your mother considered suitable friends. Where did we go for entertainment? The opera, a concert, the theater, or some other properly cultural event. Always with a group. And who made up the group? Take your pick: your brothers and their wives, your sister and her husband, their in-laws, their friends, or your visiting cousins. Sometimes your mother and some of her cronies."

"I thought you enjoyed—"

"Oh, Nick," she sighed, realizing that this was becoming the standard opening to half of her conversations with him. "I do enjoy those things occasionally. I also enjoy funny movies, the circus, ice shows, zoos, country fairs, and all kinds of other inelegant events."

"Why didn't you ever say—"

"I did. If you'll remember, there were several times we made plans to do things like that. Of course, once you'd mentioned it to your mother and the others, it always seemed there were far more important and worthwhile things to do at that time, but perhaps later . . . Except later never seemed to come."

Nick stared at her with an arrested expression and

said slowly, "Yes, *cara,* I am remembering, and you're right."

With a challenging look, Cami asked, "Are you ready for a short quiz? No pain, no strain, nothing but easy questions."

"All right."

"Name one friend we made, as a couple, who had no connection with your family."

Nick frowned and finally said, "I can't."

"When was the last time we took a vacation alone together?"

"We went skiing—" At Cami's sardonic look he sheepishly added, "With Tony and Bettina and their children."

"Can you name one time we went out by ourselves, to dinner, to lunch, to anything?"

Nick took a large swallow of his drink and stared unseeingly at the milling crowd. "Noooo...no, I can't," he admitted after a few moments. "Strange...I never realized it before."

"End of quiz," Cami said wryly, reaching for her wineglass. "Do you understand now why I asked if you were enjoying all this?"

"Mmmm...and I am. I like your friends—especially Ronan. I also like—"

"Excuse me."

Cami and Nick looked up at the young man standing at the other side of the table. His derby hat, muttonchop whiskers, and red suspenders proclaimed him a member of the jazz band.

"Yes?" Nick smiled with a questioning lift of his brows.

"Ronan says you're dynamite on the keyboards. A real pro. Our piano man is about to take a break, and we wondered if you'd like to sit in with us for a set or two."

Cami's reaction was pure shock as she gasped, "My Lord, don't you know who—"

"Sure. Sounds like fun," Nick declared, overriding her voice. The grin he gave her as he stood up was sheer deviltry. "Yes, indeed, I do believe Mother would have a terminal case of the vapors if she were here," he murmured wickedly, and he sauntered off toward the low stage at the far end of the room, leaving Cami with her mouth agape.

What does he think he's doing? When did he ever play jazz? Oh, devil take him, I wanted him to loosen up, but I didn't mean for him to come unglued!

For a few moments, until her view was blocked by the crowd, she watched the sinuous play of muscles along the length of his back and legs, clearly delineated by the snug fit of his wheat-colored jeans and matching vest. She knew that they, along with his mauve-and-blue-striped silk shirt, had been made by his favorite Italian designer. She wished the man hadn't been so precise in his tailoring. It wasn't helping her self-control to have such a graphic view of the provocatively flexing muscles of Nick's tight buttocks. She had total, vivid recall of just how they felt under her hands and just how—

"I'd go up to ten bucks to know exactly what you're thinking at this moment," Ronan's deep voice rumbled in her ear as he sat down beside her.

"Ah . . . er . . . it . . . nothing!" she squeaked, embarrassingly aware of the heat in her face.

"Never mind," Jean said from her perch on one of Ronan's solid thighs. "We can figure it out. The hot glaze of the eyes, the delicate flush on the cheeks, the half-open lips, the—"

"Stop, you goose-cap! I thought we were friends," Cami protested.

"What are friends for," intoned Jean, straight-faced,

"if not to share life's most meaningful moments?"

"Any minute now I'll give you a meaningful moment," Cami threatened as the couple broke up in laughter.

She eyed them balefully for a long second before losing control and joining in. Part of her amusement was due to the incongruous picture the two of them made. Jean was a contradiction all by herself with her combination of a definitely voluptuous body and a rounded, dimpled, scrubbed-American-girl face. Her open, forthright expression suggested a practical, conservative nature. The last woman, one would think, to be the permanent housemate of the flamboyant Ronan, with his tough, adz-carved teak face and his mysterious dark eyes that hinted of delightfully sensuous secrets.

"Where did Nick take off to?" asked Ronan, brushing the thick black curls back from his forehead and resettling his cap.

"He's gone to—what do they call it?—jam with the band."

"*Nick?*" Jean exclaimed, her blue eyes widening.

"Ask Ronan. He evidently knows something we don't," Cami complained, unthinkingly jabbing a playful elbow into Ronan's rock-hard ribs. She yelped as her arm went numb from shoulder to fingertips.

"Teach you to go beatin' on peaceable folks," Ronan chortled unsympathetically. "Matter of fact, I know a heap o' things you little gals never thought about. How to run a crane, how to pour a concrete piling, how to—Whoops! Here we go. Hush your noise now, and listen to ole Nickolai go at it."

Cami and Jean exchanged commiserating looks. Ronan, they agreed, was at his most irksome when he donned his pseudo-good-ole-boy persona.

The sound of a drum roll quieted the crowd and

directed everyone's attention to the band leader, who was waiting in front of the microphone, his trumpet tucked under his arm.

"Hope everyone's enjoying this party as much as we are," he said with an easy grin. "Where's the birthday girl? Hey there, Holly, you're lookin' good. We've got a special treat for you, honey. Seems one of your guests is a super-A-awesome piano man, and he's agreed to sit in with us for a set."

The leader half turned and flung out an arm toward Nick, seated at the piano, and exclaimed rousingly, "Ladies and gentlemen! The Down East Yankeeland Jazz Band is proud to welcome Nick de Conti!"

The audience's reaction was a mixture of astonishment—from those who knew exactly who Nick de Conti was—and anticipation—from those who knew him only as "Cami's husband who plays the piano." Before there was time for more than a patter of applause, Nick's long supple fingers were flashing over the keyboard in a dazzling, driving, intricate version of "Anything Goes." The drummer picked up the rhythm almost immediately; then, in a ripple effect, one by one the rest of the band leaped in, and they were flying.

Cami didn't realize that her mouth had dropped open until Ronan reached over and pushed it closed with his forefinger. She didn't even glance at him. She couldn't take her eyes off Nick. This was a man she had never seen before, playing as she had never heard him play before.

With his face flushed and glowing in exuberant laughter, the thick waves of his dark hair swirling around his head, and his muscles writhing with the power of his playing, Nick coaxed, challenged, and coerced the band into reaching for their limits—and then going beyond them. He led them out of "Anything Goes" into a roof-raising version of "Black Bottom Stomp" and then on, barely stopping for breath, to an incredible wails-to-whoops rendition of "Birth of the Blues."

It was one of those rare, magical times when absolutely everything worked better than it ever had before. The musicians were reading one another's minds. No sooner did one man swoop off with an improvisation on the theme than another was inspired to weave his own variation into the intricate fabric, and then suddenly they were a vital, vibrant backup as someone spiraled off and away in an inventive solo.

Cami was spellbound. She wouldn't bat an eye, at this point, if a little purple person from Pluto appeared before her and asked her to dance. Somehow in the last twenty minutes, the world had taken a ninety-degree turn, and nothing was quite where it should be. Or perhaps it was her head that was askew. She glanced down at the empty glass in her hand and wondered vaguely what had happened to her wine.

"Cami? You okay?" Ronan's deep rumble was easily heard over the cheers and clapping of the excited crowd.

"Mmmm? Oh! Yes. No. I'm not sure." Cami wondered if the impulses between her brain and tongue had been disconnected. She didn't seem to be able to say what she was thinking. She looked again at her glass and found it full.

"It's back," she said clearly, looking up at Ronan in astonishment. "Isn't that amazing?"

Jean leaned toward her and peered into her dazed eyes. "How much of that have you had, chum?"

"Not enough," Cami muttered, taking a large swallow of the wine.

Before Jean or Ronan could say anything else, there was a series of thundering chords from the piano, which was quickly joined by the other instruments as the ensemble swung into a fast, syncopated rendering of—

"Great balls of fire!" Cami gasped. "They're belting out Bach!"

She grabbed the edge of the table and pulled herself to her feet, only marginally aware of Ronan's huge hand on her back steadying her. Excitement and an electric energy were flashing back and forth between the musicians and the ecstatic crowd. Caught up in the joy of the audience, Cami started to clap and almost spilled the rest of her wine. After a moment's thought, she efficiently gulped it down and carefully set the empty glass on the table. With a triumphant grin at Jean and Ronan, she began enthusiastically clapping, more or less in rhythm with the band.

Soaring on a wine high and infected by the exhilaration of the people and the music, Cami muzzily decided to think about deeper meanings later. She joined in the wild applause when the musicians paused to catch their breath, and she whooped along with the audience when Nick swung into the next number. She wasn't the least surprised this time when she recognized it as something Nutcrackerish by Tchaikovsky.

Swinging and swaying happily, albeit none too steadily, she was rocked backward by the enthusiastic cheers of the crowd, and then almost toppled over the other way when Ronan roared, "Go get 'em, Nick!" from a foot above her head. Only his firm grip on her waist kept her upright.

Taking another swallow from her self-replenishing wineglass, and putting her trust in Ronan's supporting hand, Cami gave herself up to the sparkling pink fog and the blood-pounding rhythm.

When Nick made his way through the appreciative throng thirty minutes later, he found Cami and Jean intently discussing the aesthetic appeal of "jazzed-up Chovsky" and whether it was possible to teach fairies in toe shoes to jitterbug. He cocked an amused eyebrow at Ronan as he took in the interesting grouping. The big man was slouched back in a sturdy chair, his spread thighs providing solid perches for Cami and Jean, who were, of necessity, conducting their debate practically nose-to-nose. Ronan winked back at Nick as his chest shook with a muted rumble of laughter.

"Sloshed to the ears, the both of 'em," he replied to Nick's unspoken question. "I do believe yours is a shade more pie-eyed than mine, but there's not a whole hell of a lot to choose between them."

"I knew we were really flying there," said Nick with a rueful smile, "but I didn't think we were that devastating."

"You were fantastic, and that's just the trouble. I got distracted with the music and forgot to keep track of how much these two were putting away. A couple of guys keep coming by with wine jugs and topping off everyone's glass. I doubt if our looped ladies have any idea how much they've had."

Nick leaned down and tipped Cami's face up to his as he said softly, "Hi there, elf. Did you like the music?"

She squinted to bring him into focus, and recognition dawned. With a happy smile, she exclaimed, "Hey, it's Nicky Nimber Fingles! You were marv'ous. A'sootly marv'ous." She erupted into giggles and sputtered, "O' Lucy-goosey gonna lay bi-i-i-ig bird she hears 'bout you bombin' Bach and soupin' up the Crackernut fairies. Bet that Chovsky guy is standin' on 'is head."

"Keebler," Jean announced, tugging at Cami's skirt to get her attention.

"Who's he?" Cami asked, staring owl-eyed at her friend.

"Cracker-maker," said Jean, nodding wisely. "Soup 'n' crackernuts. Mus' be Keebler. Maybe Chovsky does soup?"

"Maybe we'd better get these two out of here," Nick gasped, his chest heaving with laughter. *I wouldn't have believed this if I hadn't seen it. My Cami, who thinks four drinks in an evening mark the road to dissipation!*

"Ayuh," agreed Ronan. "We'd better tote 'em. I doubt they could find the floor if they were lying on it."

Nick scooped Cami up in his arms and headed for the door, glancing back to see Ronan following with a giggling Jean cradled against his broad chest. Cami and Jean waved gaily in response to various "Good nights" and "See you tomorrows" as the men weaved their way across the room.

Nick and Ronan paused as a laughing blond woman intercepted them. "Good heavens, what have you done to them?" she asked, looking from Cami to Jean.

"They're a tad over the happy line," said Ronan, smiling broadly. "Nothing we can't handle. Great party, Holly."

"Thanks, but Nick's the one who made it really special," she said, turning to grin up at him. "That was a fabulous birthday present, Nick. I'll treasure the memory. Thank you so much."

"S'okay," cried Cami merrily, unwrapping one arm from around her husband's neck and reaching out to pat Holly's blond curls. "Ole Nicky Fimmer Nibbles jus' chock o' nuts wi' s'prises. Not ev'n 'is wife knows 'em all! You b'lieve that? S'true. Hey! Gimme back finga!"

Cami had managed to tangle her fingers in Holly's hair, and it took another few moments and much laughter before she was freed. Nick and Ronan made hasty farewells and strode toward the door, their ladies lustily disharmonizing on a mangled but still recognizable rendition of "We're Off to See the Wizard."

"Does Jean do this often?" asked Nick as he settled comfortably in the back seat of Ronan's station wagon with Cami snuggled in his lap.

"Never. Cami?" Ronan stopped trying to prop Jean upright in the passenger seat and let her curl up with her head on his thigh.

"First time I've ever known her to take more than three drinks." Nick tipped Cami's head back against his shoulder and tapped her cheek to see if she was awake. "Lord, but she's funny. Wonder if they'll remember any of this in the morning."

Cami blinked up at the hazily familiar face above her. "S'okay. Naughty Nicky, keepin' sec'ets." She reached up to pat his cheek and clipped him on the nose. "I forgive you. That jivin' Chovsky's kinda fun. Poor fairies gonna get sore toes. Nicky kiss 'em better. Real . . . good . . . at kissin' . . . stuff . . . better . . ."

Cami's head slid into the hollow of his shoulder, and she began to snore. Nick gazed down at the top of her head, feeling the feathery brushing of her curls against his jaw, and a surge of protectiveness welled up from somewhere deep inside him. She was his, to love and cherish, and never again would he forget that. Now if he could only regain her trust and overcome her stubbornness about going home, everything would be fine.

"You need any help?" Ronan asked as he stopped the car at the end of Cami's walk.

"No, thanks. I can manage. See you tomorrow sometime."

Cami drifted up to a fuzzy half-awake state and opened one eye a tiny slit. It was okay. Nick was carrying her home. It was a lovely way to travel, but steps weren't so good. She tightened her arms around his neck as Nick shifted his hold in order to open the screen door to her small porch.

"Easy, Cami. Let go of my neck for a minute. I've got to put you down so I can get the door unlocked. Here, sit down."

She couldn't open her eyelids beyond the halfway point, and her legs were going in different directions, so maybe it would be better if she did sit down on this nice handy suitcase. Or that one. Or the big one. My, what a lot of suitcases. Where did they—

"Am I goin' some'ere, Nicky?"

"Only to bed, elf."

"Oh. Not my soo'cases."

"No, my pickled poppet, they're mine."

"Naughty Nicky doin' no-nos. Can' stay here. Sleepin' 'lone."

"Not anymore, *cara*. I've decided it's time to move along to Act Two of this crazy operetta."

"Wha' ope'tta?"

"Mmmm. I think I'll call it 'The Courting of Lady Laughing Eyes.'"

— 6 —

CAMI SLOWLY, VERY SLOWLY, drifted up from the
depths of dreamless sleep. Her initial impressions were
all physical and all confusing. She was damp and hot
and trapped. Her head was at a strange angle. She
couldn't move one arm, and her other arm was lying
on something furry and alive. Her leg was tangled
with other, hairier legs, and her thigh was pressed
against a hard, hot—

"Nick?" It was a barely audible croak from a mouth
that felt as if that live, furry something had been
nesting in it.

"I trust you weren't expecting to wake up with
another man in your bed," Nick said in a distinctly
amused voice.

He stroked a soothing hand over the tensed muscles
in her bare back and turned his head to kiss the damp
skin at her temple.

"Relax, *cara*, and stop squirming before you over-
load my self-control. Although your hot little body
may be willing, I rather doubt that your head is ready
for a morning romp."

131

Cami froze, and her rapidly awakening mind registered a number of pertinent facts all at once. She was naked. Nick was naked. She was hot because she was pressed full-length against his exceedingly warm body, her head on his shoulder, her arm across his chest, and her legs tangled with his. One of his big hands was gently kneading her bottom, while the other one was stroking her arm. And his hands weren't all that was moving. She held her breath and ever so slightly shifted her right leg.

Blast and damn! It hadn't been a dream. *Or wishful thinking?* whispered a tiny voice. Cami quelled the voice and tried, unsuccessfully, to force her mind to logical thought. There had to be a way out of this. She wasn't ready...Well, *that* might not be entirely true, she thought, as she acknowledged the heated, moist spasms deep within her body.

Instinctively, hardly conscious of what she was doing, she moved her leg, pressing her thigh more firmly against the hardness of Nick's aroused manhood. Urged on by his hand on her rump, she thrust her pelvis forward, rubbing herself against the smooth, sensitive skin of his hip.

This was more than mortal man should be asked to stand, Nick decided as his good intentions rapidly chased his control into limbo. He had waited long enough—too damn long—for his skittish lady love to forget this platonic nonsense and get back to serious lovemaking. She'd been driving him wild for days with every enticing wriggle of her firm, rounded bottom and every suggestive motion of her small, up-thrusting breasts. But now the waiting was definitely over. She was every bit as hot for him as he was for her. She was practically scorching the skin from his hip, and he could think of much more interesting places...oh, yes.

"*Cara*, now..." he groaned as he turned to face

her, wrapped his arms around her, and rolled to pull her beneath him. "Open to me, *carissima* . . . ahhh . . . oh, yes," he whispered against her neck as he felt her legs slide up and around his hips.

His breathing deteriorated to hoarse gasps when she cradled him in the searing, slick softness between her legs. Remembering how tight she'd been the last time despite her eager participation, he forced himself to slow down long enough to arouse her to the boiling point. With a subtle flexing of his hips, he rubbed his velvet-sheathed hardness slowly and rhythmically against her soft, silken flesh until she was writhing under him, her fingers clenching into the taut muscles of his buttocks.

"Nick . . . love . . . oh, now, now . . . in me . . . now, please . . . Nick . . ." Her husky moans were interspersed with his whispered Italian urgings. She was on fire, aching, opening for him. She felt him lift his hips, and she slid her hand between their bellies, grasping him, guiding him. Her arms and legs locked around him, straining to pull him closer and deeper, abetted by his urgent hands lifting her to him.

She wasn't going to let him take it slowly, and he readily answered her gasping pleas and tugging arms, deepening and speeding up his thrusts. Her supple body twisted and flexed as his smooth strokes filled her and stretched her, building the hot, sweet tension until it burst in a kaleidoscope of blazing, shimmering colors. She was only dimly aware of his hoarse, triumphant cry as his last strong thrust locked him deep within her.

It was several minutes before Nick came to enough to realize that Cami's struggle for breath had more to do with his weight on her than with the residue of passion. He untangled himself and stretched out on his side next to her, stroking a gentling hand over her warm, damp body.

She turned her head, blinked open languid eyes, and caught her breath at the look of love on his face.

"My lady love," he whispered, his voice still husky from passion. "Are you all right? I didn't hurt you, did I?" He kissed the fingers she stroked across his lips, smiling at her expression of smug female amusement. "You're almost as tight as you were in the beginning, you know. It does terrible things to my control. Not that I'm complaining, mind you, but—"

Cami growled and rolled onto her side, pressing her naked body against his furry torso and nipping gently at his neck. "What control, you sexy piano-thumper? You've barely managed two weeks, and here you are." She wiggled a hand between their hips and sought the source of growing pressure against her belly. "Oh, my, you certainly are," she groaned, her gurgle of laughter muffled against his neck.

Why am I laughing? Blast the man! I swore we weren't going to do this until we had things settled. How did he get in here? Last night I...last night?...jazz and Nick and...fairies?...Omilord, I couldn't have!...How much wine did I drink? Nick carried me...and there were suitcases somewhere ...and I woke up naked in bed with him. My bed? Hmmm, my bed.

"Nick, wait... Ah, you sneak, stop that for a minute."

"Only for a minute, *cara*. What's the matter?"

Nick tipped her head back, smiling seductively into her scowling eyes. He closed his hand over her breast, brushing a gentle finger back and forth across the nipple, and watched her mouth open with a quickly indrawn breath.

"Your minute's almost up," he reminded her.

"We...we have to talk...and I can't when you're ...doing...doing that."

"I'm not doing *that,* sweet elf. You are. Don't you

know what your own hands are doing? Ah! Not so tight. Slower, slower, *cara*, make it last this time."

He closed his arms around her and rolled onto his back, bringing her with him and settling her astride his hips. "How's your head?" he asked, laughing up at her. "Dizzy? Aching? I'll bet I can make it feel much better in just a few moments."

"Braggart," she gasped, and then moaned a long-drawn "oooohhhh" as his big hands cupped her bottom, lifting her and fitting her down over his pulsing staff.

She braced her hands against his chest, digging her fingers into the thick curls, as her hips picked up the slow, surging rhythm from his guiding hands. Bending forward, she flicked her tongue over and around his nipples, letting her hands stroke down over his ribs to trace patterns on the sensitive skin of his abdomen. She could feel his heat rising to match the flames licking up from her vitals, fed by the increasingly urgent thrusts filling her to the point of pleasure-pain. She arched back, twisting and rocking against him in a wild seeking. Her grinding hips drove down against his suddenly strong surges, and she clamped her deep muscles around him as she felt the sense-stunning magic of their mutual climax.

Cami collapsed into Nick's arms and lay in a boneless, panting heap on his chest. The bracing early-morning breeze coming in the open windows carried the salty tang of the bay and the raucous screeling of the breakfast-seeking gulls. Cami shivered as the cool air swept across her overheated body, and Nick stretched a long arm out to reach the tumbled bedclothes. His other arm remained securely around Cami, foiling her attempts to slide off his chest.

"Stay right where you are, little one. *Now* we're going to talk."

"What you mean is that now that you've had your

way, you're going to be all kinds of magnanimous and let me have mine," drawled Cami, lifting her head to give him a knowing look. "Big of you, you impossible chauvinist, but it's not—"

"I think I liked it better last night," he interrupted, his plaintive tone belied by the laughter in his eyes, "when you were calling me Nicky Nimber Fingles."

"*Nicky?*" she gasped, her eyes wide with shock. "Me? I called you Nicky? I couldn't have! I've *never* called you Nicky."

"You never called me Nimber Fingles either."

"Nicky Nimber Fingles? I really said that? My stars and garters, how much did I drink?"

"Enough to fracture the English language into bite-sized pieces," he assured her gleefully. "I wish Ronan had gotten a recording of you and Jean discussing, with complete seriousness, how one would go about teaching the Crackernut fairies to jitterbug in toe shoes."

"I don't think I want to hear any more," moaned Cami, burying her face in his neck. "I've never been drunk in my life."

"You weren't quite that bad. Just—what's that historical phrase?—a bit on the go? Or perhaps delightfully tiddly would be more apt."

Cami braced her forearms on his chest and scowled down at his smug grin. "If that's a multiple choice . . . Oh, drat. I don't believe it. Nicky Nimber Fingles?"

"You'll never hear the end of it, *cara.*"

"Hmmm, I'll bet," she said absently as another vague memory intruded. She looked at him questioningly. "Suitcases. Do I remember something about suitcases?"

"Probably. You were sitting on one. Gavin left them on the porch, since he didn't have a key."

She stared at him, waiting.

"Yes. Well. It's no use looking at me like that," he said with a faint touch of defensiveness. "I've decided that we've had enough of dating and chastity, and since you won't move in with me, I'm moving in with you. Have moved in. And I'm staying right here until you decide to live with me again. And I'm not going to listen to any arguments about it, Cami."

Shaking her head in exasperation, she said mockingly, "Awesome, de Conti. The way your logic works is truly awesome. You're going to live with me until I decide to live with you. Not only that, but you're going to do this living in what amounts to a three-room apartment."

"Don't forget your crazy porch."

"By all means, let's not forget the porch. You've got crickets in your cadenza, maestro. The only time you've ever lived in three rooms was in a suite in a five-star hotel, and then you were waited on hand and foot. What are you going to do here? Remember, my elegant darling, there's no pool, no sauna, no Jacuzzi, no game room, no music room, no recording facilities, and *no piano*— or any room to put one."

Nick gave her a maddeningly insouciant grin and said blithely, "It won't kill me to rough it for a few weeks."

Cami ground her teeth and made a determined effort to wriggle off him, forgetting that she had comfortably nestled her legs between his. Nick seemed to like her very well right where she was, and he quickly trapped her legs with his and locked his hands behind her hips. She subsided in the face of superior strength and confined her rebellion to glowering at him.

"Don't be a dolt," she scoffed. "The closest you ever came to roughing it was getting stuck with an unheated dressing room in Moscow."

"Smile for me, Lady Laughing Eyes, and stop worrying about minor details. It will be a second honeymoon. Just you and me and—"

"And the shop and Jean and Ronan and—"

"All right, all right. A part-time second honeymoon. You did say, didn't you, that I should learn how real people live. So we'll make do with three rooms, and you can teach me to cook. Then maybe you'll stop calling me a chauvinist!"

"But, darling Nick," she gasped, laughing, "didn't you know that one of the ultimate marks of male chauvinism is the firm belief that men are naturally better cooks than women? After all, look at the ratio of male chefs to female chefs in the world's great restaurants. Ow! Don't pinch me there!"

Nick spread his hand over her left buttock and began massaging away the sting. A second later his other hand covered the back of her head, urging her to bring her mouth within reach of his.

"Oh, no!" yelped Cami, straining back against the pressure of his hand. "You can't kiss me! I haven't brushed my teeth."

He growled something short and pithy-sounding in a language she didn't recognize, then added in basic English, "You silly twit! What have your teeth got to do with anything? Is that why you kept turning away when I tried to kiss you? Is this some new fad? If you kiss before brushing, your fingernails fall off? I seem to recall many a morning I woke you up with a kiss, and you've still got all your nails and eyelashes and earlobes. Women! You get—"

"I get really nasty when rotten-tempered men yell at me before breakfast," she warned with a feral smile. "Remember, my heedless nodcock, you're in a rather dangerous position," she purred as she moved her leg suggestively against his most vulnerable appendage.

"Mmmmm . . . maybe there's something to be said

for aggressive women after all. Do it some more, you wicked elf," he urged huskily.

"I don't believe you!" she groaned in mock despair as she felt the unmistakable evidence of his reawakened passion against her thigh. "Whoever dubbed that actor the Italian Stallion has obviously never met you!"

As Nick shook with a burst of laughter, Cami took quick advantage of his relaxed grip and scrambled away from him and off the far side of the bed. Still laughing, he lunged for her, but she dodged away.

"Not now," she protested. "I've got to open the shop this morning. Besides," she teased, "I'm not sure that *three* times before breakfast is good for you."

Sprawled across the bed, leaning on one elbow in a pose made famous by Burt Reynolds, Nick gave his wife a look that should have straightened every curl on her head as he crooned, "But, *carissima*, it would be *very* good for *you*. The first two times just took the edge off. This time we could go slowly, enjoy touching and tasting, savor—"

"Stop," she groaned, backing toward the door on reluctant feet. His enticingly seductive voice and suggestive words filled her mind with an almost irresistible vision of one of their most imaginative nights of lovemaking. The temptation to leap back into his arms was strong, but she was determined that this time around Nick wasn't going to control her with magnificent bouts of lovemaking alternated with periods of benign neglect. Now he was on her territory, and they were going to play the game by her rules.

"I'm going to brush my teeth," she said firmly, grabbing a short cotton robe from a hook on the back of the door. "Then I'll go down and start breakfast while you shower. And by the way, you lazy stud, be sure you pick up these clothes you threw all over the room. There are plenty of hangers in the closet, and the laundry goes down the chute next to the bathroom door."

She sternly suppressed the nearly overwhelming need to collapse into giggles at the incredulous expression on his face. Not daring to test her control further, she quickly turned and skipped down the hall, calling back, "Better hustle your butt out of that bed. Breakfast's in twenty minutes."

Nick spent five of those minutes trying to figure out what to do with his pants. He vaguely remembered that Gavin had some kind of special hangers for them, but he couldn't find anything that seemed appropriate in Cami's dressing room. He finally draped them over the back of a chair and hoped for the best. After hanging up his vest and dumping everything else down the laundry chute, he tackled the problem of clean clothes.

"I don't see what's so difficult about this," he muttered, turning to the still unpacked suitcases he'd lugged up the night before.

Glancing around the huge closet–dressing room with its nooks and crannies containing a variety of built-in drawers, shelves, and hanging rods, he grunted in satisfaction at the sight of a long, sturdy bench against one wall. In moments he had all three suitcases open on the bench. Feeling quite pleased with himself and his newly discovered efficiency, he located his large, custom-made, leather traveling kit; then rummaged through the cases until he found underpants, socks, a pair of pale blue designer jeans, and a navy and white striped polo shirt. It took a few more minutes of hunting before he discovered his white tennis shoes in a side pocket of the largest bag.

"So much for not being able to dress without Gavin's help," he said smugly as he gathered up an armload of clothes and his travel case and headed for the bathroom.

Showered, shampooed, and shaved, Nick trotted downstairs twenty minutes later and followed the smell of coffee and bacon to the kitchen. He hadn't been in it before, and his first encompassing look brought him to a dead halt two steps into the room.

"I know you said it was weird, but this is ridiculous," he exclaimed as his gaze met Cami's laughing eyes, and he began chuckling. "Who designed it—Susan Anton?"

"Or someone at least as tall," said Cami.

Nick took another, closer look at the working area. The counters, appliances, and wall cabinets were arrayed in an L-shape along two walls, and everything had been customized to be at a comfortable height for someone no shorter than five-ten. Dropping his gaze to the floor, Nick laughed as he saw why his petite wife seemed to have suddenly grown several inches.

"Very clever," he said, nodding at the three-foot-wide by six-inch-high sections of wood-slated platforming, commonly used in greenhouses, that Cami had placed to make a raised walkway along the base of the work area.

"I had to do something. I could practically rest my chin on the counter," she said as she turned back to the stove to flip the bacon. "Breakfast will be ready in a few minutes. Why don't you have a seat?" she suggested, motioning toward the semicircular breakfast nook built into a wide bay window.

Nick slid along the seat until he had a clear view out the window. "This is rather nice. Enjoy a leisurely breakfast and watch the boat traffic on the bay. What are we having, love? Mrs. Winthrop, the Cattons' cook, does marvelous things with breakfast crepes and omelets, and she makes terrific croissants. Serves them with a peach preserve and—"

"Dream on, de Conti," Cami said sardonically. "Reality is scrambled eggs, bacon, and toast. I did gussy up the eggs a bit with some sharp cheese and cayenne, but that's the limit of my gourmet resources this morning."

Nick was lingering over his second cup of coffee when Cami slid out of the nook and began gathering up the dishes. Expecting almost anything now from his determined darling, he was only mildly surprised when she suggested that he rinse the dishes and stack them in the dishwasher while she showered and dressed.

"That doesn't sound too difficult," he murmured as he looked around the kitchen and identified the stove and refrigerator. "Ah ... where's the dishwasher?"

With her air of long-suffering patience slightly diluted by her glee, Cami got him started and then scurried upstairs with several fingers crossed for the survival of her favorite stoneware. When she returned sometime later, her glee had crystallized to vengeance.

Nick glanced up from his perusal of a price book for old bottles. "Ready to go, elf? What's on the agenda for today?"

"*I'm* ready to go. *You're* not budging out of this house until you've picked up that mess you left upstairs," she announced uncompromisingly.

Frowning slightly, he thought back over his earlier activities. Perhaps he hadn't been as efficient as he thought, but surely she couldn't be this upset over a pair of pants.

"I'm sorry, *cara,* but you didn't seem to have any hangers for pants. I didn't think you'd mind so much if I left them on the chair, but—"

"Pants? What pa—Oh, those. That was the only neat thing you did, you sloth. What about the contents of three suitcases that are strewn from one end of the closet to the other? What about the mess in the bathroom?" she yelped, flinging out her arms in exasperation. "How can it take two large bath towels and a bath sheet to dry one body? And then you left them all in damp heaps on the floor among puddles of water. The soap was all yucky from being left in the shower drain, and how did you manage to get soapsuds on the mirror over the sink? It's around the corner from the shower!"

"I . . . er . . . it wasn't—"

But Cami was in full spate and easily drowned him out. "Don't you ever put the caps back on anything? Toothpaste? Shampoo? After shave? Gad, does Gavin even scrub your back? And that's another thing; you didn't rinse the soap out of the bath brush or the washcloth, which you left on the floor of the shower. Really, Nick, it's worse than sharing a bathroom with a seal!"

A seal? No, don't ask, de Conti. Just calm her down and promise her anything before she tosses you out on your rump.

Nick wrapped his hands around her small waist and swung her up onto the walkway, where he didn't have to bend so far to kiss her. He held the back of her head in one large hand, preventing her from evading his mouth. Her tirade faded to wordless mumbles as he covered her lips with his and slid his tongue slowly and caressingly into her warm mouth. He alternately teased and taunted her until she relaxed and wound her arms around his neck, flicking her tongue against his in answering play.

Finally he drew back a few inches and looked at her contritely. "I'm really sorry about the mess, *cara*. You're right about Gavin's picking up after me all the time. I've never even thought about it, and, since we always had separate bathrooms, you never had reason to mention it before. But I'm not precisely stupid, so if you'll tell me what you want me to do, I'll clean everything up. Wring out, recap, and hang up. Okay?"

"Okay," she said slowly, watching him suspiciously. *He's plotting something. I can tell by the way his lips are twitching. Ole Nicky Nimber Fingles is going to wangle his way out of this. I'd bet my best bustle he'll be on the phone to Gavin as soon as I'm out the door.*

"Tell you what, maestro," she said, summoning up a charming smile. "Why don't you take the rest of the morning to get settled in, and I'll be back to pick you up at noontime. That is, if you'd like to go to an auction with me this afternoon?"

"An auction? Here?" Nick asked in some amazement. He wondered when Sotheby Parke Bernet had opened a Portland branch—and why.

Cami cocked her head and looked at him quizzically for a few seconds before she recalled his basic frame of reference. Chuckling, she explained, "It may come as something of a shock, my overprivileged darling, but there are thousands of auctions in this country that are *not* conducted by Sotheby's or Christie's. Today, for example, there's an auction of the contents of an old farmhouse and barn out in Gorham. It's just the sort of place that's prime hunting grounds for the shop. So, do you want to come along or not?"

"I wouldn't miss it." He gave an assessing look at her white cotton-knit shirt and green skirt with its scattering of large white polka dots and asked, "Are you going to change? Do you want me to lay out something else for you?"

"I'm fine in this. So are you. One does not wear black tie and Dior to a farm auction," she said with obvious amusement. "You'd better find a hat, though. That sun is murder when you're standing in it for several hours."

She stepped off the platform and started for the door. "See you later, Nick. You'll find plenty of empty drawers in the closet and—"

Nick hooked a long arm around her middle and swung her back onto the walkway with a decided thump. Some things, he determined, were going to be done his way. He met her startled eyes and gave her a slow, suggestive smile.

"Aren't you forgetting something?" he asked, running his tongue-tip across his lips in a blatant invitation and bringing his mouth to within an inch of hers.

Mentally throwing up her hands, she leaned forward that inch and captured his tongue between her parted lips, following its teasing flicks into the heated mystery of his mouth. Her hands tightened on his shoulders and began sliding around to explore his back as she lost herself in fevered arousal. She felt his hands closing around her waist, and she leaned into them, only to feel herself being swung through the air again.

"What—Oh!" She stared up at him, disconcerted to find herself suddenly standing in the middle of the kitchen and four feet away from him.

"You wouldn't want to be late opening, now would you?" he said with an innocuous smile. "Unless—"

"Never mind, you miserable tease," Cami purred. "I'll get you for that later."

"Great! I'll provide the champagne; you bring the oysters," he called after her as she grabbed her bag and dashed out the door.

He could still hear her trailing laughter as he reached for the phone and started dialing.

"Gavin? Would you mind coming up here right away? I seem to have a bit of a problem."

"I've got eight hundred. Do I hear nine? Nine? Nine, sir, thank you. Now ten, now ten. Do I hear ten? Ma'am? Let's hear ten, folks. This is a beautiful piece in fine condition. Not many Atlantic Grand stoves left. It's worth much more than ten, folks. Ten, I've got ten from the right, and you, sir, now eleven, eleven, let's have eleven. Eleven, thank you. Now twelve, now twelve, come on, people, let's hear twelve, twelve. It's a steal at twelve. Twelve, from the gentleman in the back. Thank you..."

"Nick! What are you doing? Put your hand down!" Cami yelped, tugging on his arm.

"I thought you wanted it," he said, distracted for the moment from the bidding.

"Not at that price," she explained quickly. "We can't affort it and—"

"Is that all?" he chided, glancing up and waving his hand again. "I can."

"...thank you, sir. I've got fifteen, do I hear sixteen, sixteen, anyone? You, sir, on the right, are you all done at fifteen? Missing out on a fine buy. Madam? Sixteen, folks, an Atlantic Grand in prime shape for just sixteen hundred dollars. It's a steal, a real..."

"Blast and botheration! You'd better pray for someone to top you," muttered Cami. "Don't you understand? I don't want the damn thing for myself. It's for the shop, and we have to sell at a profit. This is—"

"...sixteen on the right. Thank you, ma'am. Now seventeen, seventeen..."

"Don't you dare, Nick!" Cami hissed, grabbing for his arm and missing.

"...and I have seventeen from the gentleman in the back. Thank—"

"No!" Cami yelled, finally catching Nick's hands and quickly wrapping her fists around his little fingers. "If you say one word," she snarled, "I'll break both these fingers!"

"Do I have seventeen? Ma'am? Is that you, Miss Anders?"

"Yes. I mean, no, you don't have seventeen. I'm sorry, Mr. Maltan, it was an accident." Cami gave the middle-aged auctioneer her most charming smile. "He was brushing away a fly and—"

A ripple of laughter went through the crowd. Cami blushed as Mr. Maltan grinned and tipped his well-worn straw cowboy hat, drawling, "That's quite all right, ma'am. These things happen. Perhaps you'd better explain to your friend, though, the danger of waving at flies in the middle of an auction." He waited for the laughter to fade and then continued, "Back to seventeen, folks. Do I hear seventeen, seventeen . . ."

Cami released Nick's fingers and grabbed his wrist instead, pulling him after her as she edged out of the crowd and headed for the shade of a large maple tree.

"All right, *cara,* now what did I do? I thought you wanted that thing, and I—"

She heaved a gusty sigh and reached up to place a silencing finger across his lips. "Shh. It's not your fault. I forgot that you didn't have any training in the world of profit motives or the practice of buy-low-sell-high."

She glanced over her shoulder to see what was coming up next. Farm tools. Good. That would keep them busy for a while, she knew. Turning back to Nick, she said firmly, "Pay attention, now. You're about to have the world's most concise course on how to make money in the antiques business, followed by a brief exposition on strategy and game-playing at country auctions."

Fifteen minutes later, when Nick followed Cami back to her carefully chosen spot in the crowd, he'd gained a new respect for the scope of her knowledge— and an amused appreciation of her unexpected streak of Yankee-peddler shrewdness. He decided to leave the business end of things to her, but he still had a hankering to buy something himself. That little taste of bidding had been fun, and he wanted to try carrying one all the way to the end. There had to be something here Cami would like for herself, but—He stared at the far end of the piazza and smiled. He knew she loved Victorian wicker, and if he wasn't mistaken, that was a lovely old wicker étagère tucked behind that stack of planters.

"Cami, how do I pay for something? I notice that no one is collecting money."

She looked at him questioningly but answered, "See those two women at that table? You go speak to them and establish credit. Oh, lordy, how are you—"

"No problem. I've got a couple thousand in traveler's checks in my wallet. It's Gavin's idea of mad money," he said, chuckling at the look on her face as he walked away.

"It's not safe to let you out alone," Cami moaned, slumping in the driver's seat of the truck while waiting for the traffic to move.

"I wasn't alone, elf," protested Nick. "You were right there beside me."

"And you didn't pay a bit of attention to anything I said."

"Well, since I let you buy what you wanted, I figured—"

". . . that I wouldn't mind toting a truckload of weird-and-wonderfuls home for you. What are you planning to do with all that stuff?"

"I'll think of something," he murmured.

The traffic moved forward, and Cami gained twenty feet before she had to stop again. She half turned in her seat to take a long look at her husband. She'd been so busy in the past weeks trying to stay one step ahead of him that she hadn't really assimilated the changes in him.

Now that she was looking for them, she could see any number of differences between the man sitting beside her and the one who had stormed into the shop some three weeks ago. He'd gained back a few pounds and was almost up to his normal weight. His bones no longer seemed to be coming through the skin, and his face was much less haggard. The marks of tension around his eyes and mouth had faded. As he leaned back in his seat, he looked relaxed, with no sign of the frazzled nerves that had kept his muscles in knots.

An impatient horn behind her brought her attention back to the road, and she managed almost a hundred feet this time. She slanted another look at Nick. Yes, he definitely had improved, she decided. He looked happy, satisfied. She knew he'd really enjoyed the auction, and not just because it was something different. No, he'd truly gotten into the spirit of the thing with all the delight of a small boy discovering the girl-scaring potential of frogs and worms.

What's the matter with you, you peagoose? Why are you playing Wicked Witch of the West? Isn't this what you wanted from him? Shape up, twit, and meet him halfway. He had a great time. Now don't spoil it by nagging him. What the hell! You can think of something to do with half a dozen cowbells and a boxful of old automobile radiator ornaments. And some of those things, like the music box with a dozen discs, are collector's items. Furthermore, you wimp, you haven't even thanked him for that gorgeous piece of wicker.

Thoroughly irritated with herself, Cami took a quick look around to see exactly where she was, and then flipped on the directional signal and began edging to her right. She turned down the next street on the right, then swung left after two blocks and pulled into one of the parking lots of the University of Southern Maine.

"What are we doing here?" Nick asked, gesturing at the nearly deserted lot.

He eyed his wife cautiously as she turned off the ignition and twisted around in her seat to face him. Her troubled look puzzled him, and he wondered, with a certain amount of resignation, what was coming next. He knew he was awkward at some of the things she considered important, but he was trying, dammit, and the least she could do was meet him halfway.

"Cami?"

"Oh, Nick, I'm such a goose-wit sometimes, I can't stand myself," she said mournfully. "The auction *was* fun, and here I am spoiling it for you, for us. I don't know why I'm picking at you. Some of those things you got were very good buys; several of them are collector's items."

"*Cara—*"

"Let me finish," she interrupted, reaching to pull his head down so she could feather kisses across his willing mouth. "Thank you for that fantastic étagère. The wickerwork in those back panels is some of the most original I've ever seen."

She pressed her mouth to his, deepening the kiss as his lips opened, seeking his tongue with a sudden, intense need. Then his hands were gripping her, lifting her across the gap between the seats, and settling her in his lap. He became the aggressor, sensing her need and thrusting his urgent, rigid tongue deep into her mouth, his hands stroking and kneading her pliant body.

She was deaf to anything but the sounds of their labored breathing and their wordless moans. Her breasts were firming and thrusting with desire, and she squirmed around to press them against the muscular wall of his chest, rubbing sinuously against him like a cat begging to be stroked.

He clamped one arm around her back, lifting her more tightly against him, while his other hand slid under the hem of her skirt and began nudging its way up between her thighs. She clenched her fingers into the muscles of his shoulders as passion blazed through her. His state of arousal was unmistakable, and she flexed the muscles of her buttocks as she pressed down with a slow rotation of her hips against the hard ridge of his manhood.

"You little witch, you do pick your moments," Nick groaned against her neck. "Let's get—"

"Here, now, what do you folks think you're doin'?"

A bolt of lightning couldn't have shocked them any more than the sudden sound of a harsh, aggressive voice from beside Nick's window. They jerked apart and turned to stare at the belligerent man in a security guard's uniform.

"We don't allow those kinds of carryin' on in—"

"My apologies, sir," said Nick in a voice Cami mentally described as dripping with sincerity and syrup. "My wife was suddenly overcome—with a fit of gratitude, you understand—and we felt it would be safer to get off the road before she succumbed to her . . . feelings."

"Nick! You—"

"Well, in that case, mister," mumbled the subdued guard, "since she's your wife, we can just forget it. Might be a good idea, though, to get her home before she, ah, has any more o' them fits. Ayuh."

"You're absolutely right," Nick agreed with a charming smile. He turned to Cami and said dulcetly, "Shall we go, love? I'm sure we'll be much more comfortable on the . . . turret porch."

Cami had managed to scramble back into her seat, and now she divided a smoldering look equally between the smug male grins. "By all means," she gritted, twisting the ignition key, "let's adjourn to the turret porch. Just remember, my darling beast, the higher you climb, the farther you fall . . . when I push you over the rail!"

Clamping a firm hold on her temper, Cami managed to drive sedately out of the parking lot. There was a tense, deafening silence in the truck until Nick began humming something she vaguely recognized as a popular version of a Chopin theme. After a few minutes the humming stopped, and her peripheral vision caught the movement as he half turned toward her.

"Strange, isn't it," he murmured thoughtfully, "how sexual frustration can sour the sweetest disposition."

She flashed him a quick look and noted his expression of barely suppressed laughter. It was too much. She bit her lip in consternation but finally gave up.

"Yours or mine?" she asked in a reasonably cool voice, flicking him another brief glance. That was all it took. The instant their eyes met, they began to laugh, and Cami drove toward home—and the turret porch—with growing anticipation.

7

NICK LET THE door of The Elegant Magpie swing closed behind him and threaded his way among the dozen or so customers and the free-standing display cases to the rear of the shop.

"Hi, Pat. Busy day?" he murmured to the slightly frazzled-looking young woman behind the back counter. "Ronan upstairs?"

Interpreting her distracted smile and vague wave as a yes, Nick stepped through the macrame curtain, crossed the storeroom to open an unobtrusive door, and ran up the concealed spiral staircase. Reaching the narrow landing at the top, he pressed his hand against a surprisingly sturdy steel door and turned his head to look up at the lens of a closed-circuit TV camera mounted high on the wall and positioned to give a clear view of the stairs and landing. A muted buzz, two clicks, and the door swung open, allowing him to stroll into Ronan's large workroom.

"Getting in here is almost as difficult as visiting the vaults at Fort Knox," he complained.

Ronan grinned but didn't look up from what he was doing at the high workbench. "If I had as much gold as they do, it would be just as difficult. As it is, I think the insurance people have gone whacko on the subject of alarms. I've got three separate systems, and now they want me to upgrade again with some new infrared widget. Next thing you know they're going to be after me to rig the box," he snarled, waving at the walk-in vault, "to spray unauthorized visitors with knockout gas." He picked up a jeweler's loupe and peered at the catch on a gold chain. "Pull up a stool. I'll be done in a minute."

Nick perched on a high stool, made comfortable with a padded seat and back, and relaxed in the welcome coolness of a brisk ocean breeze blowing in through the large screened windows in the north and east walls of the corner room. The thick granite walls and high ceilings of the converted warehouse also helped to keep the July heat at bay. He glanced up at the special-alloy-steel shutters above the windows and wondered what the insurance company expected in the way of attack. Relatively lightweight and easy to raise and lower, the shutters were, he knew, nonetheless impervious to just about anything but a direct hit by a fairly large artillery shell.

"Just think, Ronan," said Nick idly, "if the harborfront is ever bombarded, the building may go, but those shutters will for damn sure survive."

"Bunch of wimps," muttered the big man, standing and stretching the kinks out of his back. "There was a rep from the police department in here with that paranoid from the insurance company, and he just about swallowed his tongue when he saw the amount of gold, silver, and unset stones in the vault. Kept raving about putting the bulk of it in a bank, until I quoted the statistics on bank robberies per day in the

U.S. Enough of that. Want a cold beer? Haven't seen you all week. What's happening?"

"A beer sounds good. Thanks. Those practice rooms at the university aren't air-conditioned. I stopped by the apartment for a quick shower and change, but still..." Nick took a couple of long swallows of beer and sighed with relief. "I assume our Cami–Jean news service has kept you informed about the concert?"

"It's the wildest idea I've heard this year. Can't wait to see if you bring it off."

"What else could I do? Hell, man, the committee only found out Wednesday night that Crayle got himself clobbered in a car crash. Here they are with a sell-out concert scheduled for Saturday, and suddenly no star and no time to find another top name."

"In country rock," Ronan interjected.

"I don't think they cared much at that point," Nick said, "what kind of a performer they got, as long as it was someone those ticket-holders would sit still for."

"A big name in pop music," Ronan insisted. "You don't draw the same kind of audience. How did they get to you, anyhow?"

"Stacey Clarkson's on the committee, and she's a cousin of the Cattons. She knew I was up here for the summer and tracked me down Thursday morning, mostly to see if I could pull any strings to get them a 'name' by Saturday night. I made a few calls and came up zero, and that's when Cami and Jean had their brainstorm."

"You sure they hadn't been belting down a few at the time?"

"Cold sober, both of 'em," said Nick, laughing. "It's really not a bad idea, you know. The Civic Center's sold out, and this is about the only thing we can come up with on such short notice that just might keep half those people from claiming refunds. It should be fun."

Nick chuckled at the look on Ronan's face and wondered why he wasn't just as appalled. A few weeks ago he'd have been outraged if anyone had suggested that he give a public performance in company with a group called the Down East Yankeeland Jazz Band. But now, after almost two weeks of living in a three-room apartment with Cami and being initiated into her version of how "normal" people lived, he found that he'd changed his ideas about a lot of things, and he was actually looking forward to Saturday night's show. It *was* going to be fun, and he intended to enjoy every minute of it.

"What did that fancy manager of yours say when you told him what you were planning?" Ronan asked.

"Beats me. He kept moaning and babbling incoherently, and after five minutes I told him to call me if he had any questions, and I hung up. I haven't heard from him since."

"So how are you doing? You set this up yesterday noon. Today's Friday, and the show's tomorrow night," said Ronan seriously. "When are you going to rehearse with the band? Can you put it together this fast?"

"We had a session last night for several hours, and I've spent the morning working out a few new versions of some stuff by Ravel, Wagner, and Shostakovich. We're getting together tonight for a long session and then again in the morning. Fortunately there's nothing on at the Civic Center tonight, so we've got it for both rehearsals. I called my A-and-R man at Columbia and told him what we were doing. He's flying in this afternoon with his best sound man and a technical crew. They'll handle all the acoustics problems, and they're also going to tape the performance."

Ronan gaped at him. "Tape? To sell?"

"Who knows?" Nick grinned at him and shrugged. "If it comes off well, maybe. We'll have to see."

A shout of laughter rattled the light fixtures as Ronan collapsed onto a stool and gasped between bouts of mirth, "I can see...it now, the album ...cover saying...Nicky 'Nimber Fingles' de Conti and...the Down East Yankeeland Jazz Band... Jivin' It Up with the Crackernut Fairies...Oh, Lord, I can't stand it!"

Chuckling, Nick watched patiently until Ronan finally subsided and wiped his eyes. "It's a wonder you haven't set off all your alarms," he said dryly. "Now that you've got that out of your system, how about joining me for lunch?"

"You're on. Let me lock this stuff up first."

"This place is beginning to grow on me," Nick commented some fifteen minutes later as he looked around the cool, low-ceilinged main room of Ronan's favorite pub.

"Just one of the things you'll miss if you manage to drag Cami back to Connecticut," said Ronan with a sly look at the other man. "How's the campaign going?"

"It's not," Nick sighed. "We're getting along beautifully on all other fronts, but any mention of going back home and you can hear the mental blocks crashing into place. Damn, but she's stubborn!"

"Ayuh. I know another one just like her. I think they goad each other on. Speaking of getting along, has Cami succeeded in domesticating you yet?" Ronan asked with a too-innocent-to-be-true look.

"You heard," Nick said resignedly. "I knew Cami'd never keep it to herself."

"Cami's right, you know," chided Ronan. "You have no instinct for making money, and it's a damn

good thing you don't have to. Now there was a golden
opportunity to turn a tidy sum by selling tickets, but
did you even think of it? No, not you. You just sel-
fishly kept all the fun—"

"Fun! I'll have you know—"

"...to yourself. Of course," Ronan continued
thoughtfully, "you wouldn't have been able to get too
many people into the apartment, but you could have
at least filmed—"

"Filmed! You are definitely a few sheets short, you
crazy Gypsy, and should—"

"...it so your friends could enjoy—"

"Seeing me make an idiot of myself? Thanks a
lot," Nick said wryly. "But don't despair. The way
things are going, just stick around, and there'll be
another opportunity at any moment."

Ronan gave him an unrepentant grin and asked
conspiratorily, "Did you really flood the whole downstairs? Were the suds up to Cami's chin? Why did
you—"

Nick groaned and took a fortifying swallow of dark
beer. "I can see what kind of a story those two made
out of this. No, I didn't flood the downstairs. It was
just an excess of soapsuds...well, a whole hell of
a lot of soapsuds...and they sort of spread from the
pantry, where the washer is, across the kitchen and—
I suppose you want all the gory details?"

"Right from the horse's mouth," agreed Ronan.

"Actually, it was all Jean's fault. Cami was going
to take Monday morning off to catch up on housework
and laundry, but then Jean called and asked her to
take a fast run up to Yarmouth to pick up an old
icebox. Like a damn fool, I offered to get the housework started."

"Like any 'normal' husband?" interjected a grinning Ronan.

"Please," Nick begged with a rare touch of self-consciousness, "give me credit for trying. Anyhow, Cami already had the first load in the washer and the water running. She muttered something about adding liquid detergent and closing the cover, and then she dashed out the door. So I found the instructions on the inside of the washer cover and dumped in a cup of detergent, closed the thing up, and went upstairs to vacuum. *That* I already knew how to do, and it only took about twenty minutes. I was on my way back when I heard this odd noise from the kitchen."

"And? Come on, Nick, what happened?"

"Oh, hell, all right. There was this wave of soap-suds about two feet high slowly spreading across the kitchen floor, and the pantry seemed to be full of a huge mass of the stuff. The odd noise was coming from the washer, and I figured I'd better get it shut off. So I took my shoes off and rolled up my pant legs—not that it did much good—and waded in."

"How high was it? Did you really get buried?"

"Come on, Ronan, don't believe everything Cami tells you! Of course I didn't get buried. Well, not exactly. It was only a little above my knees in the kitchen, but in the pantry it was up to my shoulders. I remembered the instructions inside the washer's cover and lifted it up, and that turned the machine off."

"So there you were, up to your ears in soapsuds," gasped Ronan between fits of laughter, "and wondering how to get it cleaned up before Cami got back. That must have been a sight! What did you do?"

"I didn't have a chance to do anything. About then Cami came running into the house yelling for me not to start the washer because she'd forgotten to warn me about not using too much liquid detergent. She reached the kitchen door, and I wish I had a picture of her expression when she saw that enormous tide of soapsuds."

"What did she say?"

"It's not repeatable. In fact, I've been wondering ever since where she learned that expression," said Nick with an inquiring look at Ronan.

"Not from me," protested the other. "However, I might mention that Jean has a very colorful vocabulary on the rare occasions when she loses her temper. So then what happened? How did you get rid of a roomful of suds?"

"Before I had time to stop Cami, she came charging across the kitchen, but in the excitement of the moment she forgot to take off her sneakers. She made it to the door of the pantry before she slipped and went skidding out of sight under the highest part. I was trying to push the damn stuff aside with one arm while I groped around for her with my other hand. I could hear her coughing and making weird noises, and suds were flying everywhere from her waving her arms around trying to get hold of something solid. I finally managed to grab her arm just as she got a firm grip on my pant leg and tried to pull herself up."

"Don't tell me!" choked Ronan. "Instead of you pulling her up, she pulled you down and buried both of you in soapsuds. I can just picture it! Oh, Lord, why don't you do these things when I'm around?"

"With our luck," said Nick, eyeing his friend's massive proportions, "you'd end up falling on top of us and flattening us beyond recognition. Anyhow, by the time we got out of there, we were absolutely covered from head to toe with foam. We had to go outside and rinse off, clothes and all, with the garden hose."

"And what did you do about your houseful of suds?"

Nick started laughing. "Same thing...I always do...in an emergency. I called...Gavin to come and take...care of it. For once...Cami had no objections. None at all."

"Who'd have believed a cup of detergent would cause all that?" Ronan mused.

Nick debated with himself for a minute but finally confessed, "It wouldn't have if I'd used the laundry detergent. Oh, I'd have had a few extra suds, but nothing like a roomful."

"What did you use?"

Nick gave him a sheepish grin. "The first squeeze bottle I saw that said detergent. Only it turned out to be dishwashing liquid, and that, it seems, makes twenty times the suds that laundry detergent does. Will you stop bellowing, you mad Gypsy? People are staring at us."

Nick glanced up at the giggling waitress who had materialized beside the table. "Ignore him, Ruth. A couple more beers, and I'll have the mixed grill and a large salad with blue-cheese dressing. You can bring him a slab of raw steak. I'm not sure how rabid he might be, so maybe you'd better toss it to him from the middle of the room."

It was after two before Nick and Ronan ambled forth onto the sidewalks crowded with tourists visiting the intriguing shops of the Old Port. Nick derived considerable amusement from the looks his large and flamboyant friend was receiving. By now he was used to Ronan's outlandish costumes and actually felt that today's ensemble was reasonably conservative. He glanced sideways at the loose white cotton pants and the open vest of the same material. True, they were on the colorful side, with those embroidered red and green dragons romping all over them, but Nick rather thought it was that vast bare expanse of hairy chest that was causing so many older women to frown and younger ones to flutter their eyelashes.

"It's like being in a circus parade," he murmured.

"What is?" asked Ronan.

"Walking along a public street with you," Nick

answered, chuckling. "Cami's right, you know; no one pays the least attention to me, and that's just the way I like it," he added with heartfelt satisfaction. "I may take you along on tour and see if it works in the rest of the world."

"Forget it, maestro. I've got much more interesting things to do than act as camouflage for you. Why don't you grow your beard again?"

"Uh-uh. Cami didn't like it. Where are we going?" Nick asked in idle curiosity as they turned onto Fore Street.

"To see what the girls are up to. Since you're going to be rehearsing half the night, I thought I'd ask Cami if she'd like to grab a late supper with Jean and me."

"Good thinking," Nick commented. Then they started discussing plans for the following evening as their long legs quickly covered the distance to the shop.

"Hello, what's this?" Ronan muttered, pausing a step ahead of Nick at the shop door.

Peering past his shoulder, Nick read aloud from a hastily lettered sign taped to the door: "Closed for a brief emergency. Will reopen at three o'clock. Please return then." He exchanged a puzzled glance with Ronan, then leaned to look through the window. "Somebody's in there. Try the door."

Ronan pulled open the screen door and turned the handle on the inside door. "Locked. Hold on. I've got a key." He pulled a large ring of keys from his pocket, selected one, and quietly opened the door. "Make like a mouse," he whispered over his shoulder to Nick, "until we find out what's going on."

Much to Nick's amazement, Ronan's 210 pounds never made a sound as he slid swiftly through the doorway and stepped aside to give Nick room to enter. Half expecting to find Cami and Jean unconscious and a thief ransacking the place, Nick quickly scanned the shop as Ronan took two long strides to the checkout counter and glanced behind it. It wasn't until Nick turned to make a slower examination of the shop that he saw the young woman half hidden behind a display rack.

Before he could speak or move, Jean came into view, pacing distractedly from the other section of the shop, her arms folded across her chest, her head down, and muttering a steady litany of curses in three or four languages. At that moment the door to the storeroom opened, and he heard Cami's voice, angry but controlled, stating, ". . . will not listen to any more of this garbage."

He started forward, then froze as an all-too-familiar voice snapped disdainfully, "He found you in a shop, and it comes as no surprise to me that, despite my efforts to train you to be a proper wife for a de Conti, you seized the first opportunity to return to your natural milieu. I've long believed that people, like water, will seek their own level, and yours is obviously shop-keeping. You—"

"Mother!" Nick gasped, unfreezing and starting for the storeroom.

Jean's head snapped up, and she jumped in front of him, planting both hands on his chest to stop him. "Oh, no you don't, Nick!" she warned. "For once you're going to learn firsthand how your mother carries on when she thinks you're not around."

Nick stared at her and then at the open door. His first instinct was to protect Cami from his mother's scathing tongue. He'd never heard his mother speak like that. *My Lord, is this what Cami's been putting up with all along?* As he hesitated, he heard Cami's voice again, angrier now and beginning to rise.

"Aren't you forgetting, Lucianna, just how all those

marvelous de Contis piled up their millions? They were businessmen, to put it in socially acceptable terms, although there are those who would be quicker to call them robber barons. Back in those days there were very few laws to protect people from the rich and powerful. The de Contis were no better than the other clever men who grabbed thousands of acres of land, built railroads where they wanted them, forced small competitors into bankruptcy, all but stole—"

"Be silent, you unprincipled little opportunist! Don't think for a moment that I'm taken in by your juvenile rantings. You were so busy trapping my son into this disgusting marriage that you never gave a thought or cared a whit as to where all that money came from. You were too eager to get your hands on it. But I saw to it, didn't I, that you had no joy of it. The de Conti name represents a centuries-old tradition of culture and elegance, and we know how to protect it from ill-bred gold diggers. Don't think for a moment that you're the first fortune hunter we've had to send packing, and you probably won't be the last. Your only distinction, girl, is that it's taking a bit longer than usual to get rid of you, thanks to my poor, naive boy's utter blindness to your true character. But I've taken care of that. Once he sees your gaucheness against Oriana's impeccable breeding, he'll finally recognize how totally unsuited you are to the de Conti name."

Nick snarled something in Italian and started around Jean, only to be brought up short by Cami's rebuttal in a tone so cold it gave him goose bumps.

"Really, Lucianna, talk about ill-bred. You sound exactly like a screeching streetwalker defending her territory. Do try to accept, with at least a modicum of grace and good manners, the fact that Nick came after me because he wants to—"

"I'll tell you what he wants, you little fool!"

screamed Lucianna, entirely out of control. "He wants
to bring you back home, back under my guidance,
before you and your low-life friends bring some unspeakable disgrace down on our heads. Oh, you think
he's going to let you do what you want, but that won't
last long. Once he's gone on tour again—"

Nick's temper erupted. "Mother, shut up!" he
roared, striding rapidly across the shop and flinging
the storeroom door wide open.

A fast encompassing look at his wife reassured him
that, although white-faced with rage, she was in fine
fighting trim and clearly uncowed. With smoldering
charcoal eyes and a rapidly burgeoning temper, he
turned to face his mother. Nothing in all his thirty-
three years had prepared him for the bitter, sneering
virago he had heard screaming insults at his wife, and
his perception of the shocked woman now confronting
him had changed unalterably forever.

"Dominic! But I thought you were . . ." Tall, thin,
elegantly dressed in a Halston summer frock, her gray
hair artfully arranged, Lucianna de Conti stared almost
uncomprehendingly at her son as her words died under
the force of his anger.

"Yes? You thought what?" He bit the words off in
a tone of barely suppressed rage. "That I was safely
out of sight and hearing? That you could come here
and attack my wife with impunity? That I wouldn't
discover how you lied to me a few weeks ago?"

He drew in a deep breath, trying to hold on to his
temper, only marginally aware of the silent tension
emanating from his stunned audience. All his senses
were focused on his mother as he watched her attempt
to rally her forces.

"Gavin assured me," Lucianna faltered, apparently
unaware that she was giving herself away, "that you
would be practicing all day. Of course I . . . I didn't

expect—Oh, you don't understand, darling! I would never have...but I simply couldn't stand...When your wife began shouting insults at me the moment we walked in, it was more than I could bear. You know how hard I've tried to be kind and forgiving, despite—"

Nick sliced a rigid hand through the air, effectively cutting off his mother's self-pitying litany in midsentence. "I don't want to hear that drivel. I want to know what you're doing here."

"That's obvious, darling," murmured Lucianna, stepping toward him and reaching out to lay her hand on his arm. "Since you're bringing Cami home—"

She recoiled as Nick brushed her hand away and moved next to Cami, dropping a protective arm around her shoulders. "No, Mother, it's not at all obvious—unless you want me to believe that you came up here solely to antagonize my wife and to finish your nearly five-year campaign to permanently alienate us from each other."

"You didn't let me finish, Dominic," Lucianna chided, making a visible effort to modulate her tone to one of loving concern, although her dark eyes flashed balefully at Cami. "The moment Arthur told me of this appalling exhibition you're planning to make of yourself—how could you even think of doing anything so crass and tasteless?—I knew I had to come up and rescue you from these people. When Gavin said you were unavailable this afternoon, I naturally came to Cami to convince her—"

"I heard the way you were convincing her, Mother," Nick said disgustedly. "But I'm understandably puzzled as to what you were convincing her of. I'm also curious about these people you think I need to be rescued from. Do I take it that you object to my playing a jazz concert?"

"Please," his mother moaned, pressing a long, fine-boned hand to her heart. "I can't bear to hear the word. You cannot possibly do anything so ludicrous. You're the finest classical pianist in the world, Dominic. How can you even think of...of bastardizing your great talent by so much as appearing on the same stage with those revolting people, never mind actually playing with them? It would be a...an unspeakable abomination!"

Lucianna's tone of pure loathing left no doubt that Nick could not have horrified her more if he'd confessed to a desire to run out and molest children. Cami stared at her from the warm shelter of Nick's enclosing arm and felt the last of the rage that had sustained her for the past twenty minutes slowly drain away. She realized that a new feeling was swiftly replacing the deep dislike she'd long felt for her mother-in-law. It took a few confused seconds for her to recognize that new feeling for what it was.

Pity. I pity her. For the first time in Nick's life, she's let him see the ugly side of her nature. All those things she feels so strongly but has always managed to hide because she knew that the people who were important to her would find them unpleasant and unadmirable. Poor Nick, he must be devastated. Despite everything he's learned about her in the past weeks, he hung on to the belief that she loved and understood him. He was so sure that her lies and deceit were merely a misguided attempt to protect him, and he believed her promises to accept me back into the fold and to cease interfering. Oh, Nick!

Cami looked up at her husband's tense face and slid a comforting arm around his waist. It had cost him a few shattered illusions, but he'd stood by her, unhesitatingly, unequivocally, and there could no longer be any doubt in Lucianna's mind as to which of them came first with him.

Nick looked down and met his wife's understanding gaze. He felt a gradual easing of the emotional turmoil he'd been pitched into during the past few minutes. Listening to his mother and watching her bitter, disdainful expression, he'd been overwhelmed by shock, disbelief, dismay, and finally an almost sickening acceptance of the obvious fact that she was obsessed with the idea of breaking up his marriage. He squeezed Cami's shoulders in a brief, hard hug, and part of his mind became very busy sorting out some new options, while the other part centered on how to get rid of everyone so he could have an hour alone with his wife.

"After you, Mother," he said firmly, gesturing toward the door to the shop. "I think any further discussion on *any* subject would be a complete waste of time. We're obviously in total disagreement, and I don't have time for fruitless arguments."

Nick led Cami back into the shop in his mother's wake. After few steps he paused as he suddenly remembered that there'd been an audience for that ugly scene. He scanned the shop quickly. It was empty, but through the front window he could see Jean and Ronan outside talking with the young woman he'd noticed earlier.

"Nick! Quickly! Get Oriana away from those dreadful people!" Lucianna demanded as she spotted the trio outside. She started rapidly for the door, exclaiming in tones of horror, "That man looks like a *hippie!*"

Cami stiffled a giggle as she and Nick followed at a more leisurely pace. She slanted a laughing look up at Nick, murmuring, "I haven't heard that word in years. Can't you just imagine Ronan's face if she goes out there and calls him a hippie?"

"All too well," Nick growled, "which is why we'd better muzzle her before she insults one of our best friends."

He quickened his pace and reached the door just as his mother opened it, calling, "Oriana! Do come away from those—"

"That's enough, Mother," he snapped. "If you'll just stand back so everyone can come in..."

Oriana, answering Lucianna's call, stepped past Nick into the shop. He nodded to her as he motioned for Jean and Ronan to come back in, too.

"Before you go, Mother," Nick said, giving Lucianna a level look, "I'd like you to meet our friends, Jean Vernon and Ronan McBain. Jean and Cami were college roommates and are now business partners. Ronan is a very fine goldsmith." He nodded to Jean and Ronan, gesturing toward his mother. "My mother, Lucianna de Conti, and this is..." he said hesitantly, looking inquiringly at his mother.

"Really, Dominic," she said impatiently, "you can't have forgotten dear Oriana. Of course, she has grown some since you last saw her, but—"

"You must forgive me, Oriana," Nick said smoothly with a warm smile for the obviously bewildered young woman. He felt rather sorry for her. Slim, dark-haired, with a face that could most accurately be described as sweet, she was plainly mystified by both his mother's behavior and the antagonism filling the air. It was equally plain that she'd had no part in his mother's machinations, but had been brought along as an innocent pawn in Lucianna's campaign against Cami. With innate courtesy, Nick set about putting the confused young woman at ease.

"You're Oriana Antigori, aren't you? I remember now; Mother mentioned several weeks ago that your family would be visiting *I Venti di Mare* this summer. You must forgive..."

Cami let the sound of Nick's voice fade to a hum as she examined Oriana Antigori. After all the times she'd had the Italian girl's perfections and suitability thrown in her teeth, Cami had been fully prepared to dislike her thoroughly if they ever met. Now she found herself feeling nothing but sympathy for this shy, gentle girl who was as much a victim of Lucianna's obsession as Cami was.

"Cami?"

Nick's prompting brought her attention back to the moment. After another few minutes of polite chitchat, Nick was ushering his mother and Oriana outside. Cami waited with Jean and Ronan, none of them speaking, as they watched Nick exchange a few words with his mother, then glance up the street and raise his hand in a signal. Within seconds a dark blue limousine glided smoothly to the curb, and Cami recognized one of the de Conti chauffeurs.

Suddenly the significance of the farewell scene being enacted outside hit Cami, and she was filled with such a sense of joy and lightness that she looked down to make sure her feet were still on the floor.

That's it! Good-bye, farewell, and don't call us, we'll call you! No more Lucianna and her sniping and snipping—except on formal family occasions. I don't know where we're going to live—except that it won't be in Connecticut—and I don't really care as long as Nick and I are together. Really together. The way we've been these past weeks, but in a bigger place, with Gavin and a housekeeper and a cook and whatever else we need so that we can do things together when he's not practicing and I'm not working, and I can tour with him and—

"Cami! Snap out of it, *cara*. Come on," Nick said insistently, grabbing her hand and pulling her out the door behind him. "I need to talk to you alone, and I've only got an hour before I have to meet the band. It's all right," he soothed as she sputtered a protest. "Jean and Ronan will watch the shop."

* * *

"Do you remember this table?"

"It's the one we had the first night you brought me here," Cami answered a bit breathlessly. Nick had set a fast pace on their walk to Harbor House. His low-voiced conference with the maître d' had also been quick, and she'd barely had time to catch her breath before he whisked her across the nearly empty dining room and seated her at "their" table.

She met his intense gray gaze and asked hopefully, "Is this an occasion?"

"It is indeed. Oh, yes, it definitely is," he assured her in a voice husky with emotion.

She folded her hands tightly together on the edge of the table as she watched him pull out his wallet and remove a fold of tissue paper from one of the compartments. She sensed what it was, and her eyes followed each movement of his fingers as he unwrapped her wedding ring. He reached across the table and tugged her left hand free, holding it in his warm clasp and rubbing the tension from her stiff fingers with his thumb.

"Now will you wear your ring again?" he asked softly, the warm, loving look in his eyes answering the questions that no longer needed to be asked.

She swallowed hard, willing away the joyful tears before they could spill over. It wasn't the first time he'd asked her to take her ring back. She'd refused before, insisting that they had to settle *all* their differences before she'd feel right about wearing it again. But now . . .

"Oh, yes, please," she whispered, her eyes shimmering with tears.

"I love you, my Lady Laughing Eyes," he said with a catch in his voice as he slid the band of small emeralds onto her finger once more.

"And I..." She hesitated as a marvelous thought popped into her mind, and then smiled beguilingly at him. "And I love you, my Lord Nimber Fingles!"

...And They Lived
Snappily Ever After!

"CAMI? CAMI!"

"You bellowed, maestro?"

Cami propped herself up on her elbows and blinked sleepily, bringing Nick's rapidly striding figure into focus. Feathers of sand flew from beneath his feet as he crossed the small private beach, and his thick hair billowed around his head in the breeze of his passage.

"You're going to ruin those shoes, tramping through the sand in them," she commented as he came to a halt beside her beach towel, planted his fists on his hips, and glared down at her impatiently.

"What are you doing down here? It's after three."

"I *was* taking a nap," she murmured, rolling to a sitting position. She let her eyes travel slowly from his handmade English shoes, up the length of the elegant silk-and-wool-blend pale gray trousers, across the bare, furry chest, and over his scowling face before meeting his stormy gaze.

She smiled seductively and quirked an eyebrow, purring, "Love your outfit. You're going to knock the socks off those starchy old broads on the concert committee. Maybe you'd better jot down the number of the cardiac emergency unit."

"Very funny," Nick growled. "Where the hell is Gavin? He's got half my stuff packed, and the other half's at the cleaners. I can't find anything!"

Laughing, Cami held up a hand so he could pull her to her feet. "He's taking her royal mini-highness for her afternoon perambulation." She picked up her towel, shook it free of sand, and tossed it over her arm. "I'll come up with you and find a shirt. It's probably right under your nose."

"Maybe there's not all that much hurry," murmured Nick, his eyes starting to glint as they skimmed over his wife's enticing body, which was barely concealed by her minuscule red and gold bikini. "Why is Gavin walking the baby when he should be finishing my packing?" he asked absently. "What are we paying that incredibly expensive genuine English nanny for?"

Cami grabbed a large wandering hand and tugged her husband firmly toward the steps. "I believe this afternoon's walk—it is Wednesday, isn't it?—yes, well then, this afternoon's walk is devoted to the study of ornithology, and that incredibly expensive genuine English nanny is, according to Gavin, woefully lacking in her knowledge of North American birds."

Nick pulled Cami to a halt at the foot of the steps and stared at her disbelievingly. "Birds? For heaven's sake, Abby's only eight months old!"

Starting up the steps, Cami grinned back at him over her shoulder. "Gavin says it's never too soon to start teaching children an appreciation—"

Nick cut her off with an untranslatable Italian phrase, but then became momentarily sidetracked watching the gentle swing of her hips as she climbed the stairs ahead of him. Cami glanced back at him

and laughed, skipping out of reach along the board-
walk that led across the dunes from the steps to the
gate in the high mesh fence surrounding the landscaped portion of their grounds.

Cami turned at the gate and looked out over the
ocean, blue and serene under a cloudless sky on this
lovely mid-September afternoon. "It's so beautiful,"
she said softly, slipping an arm around Nick's bare
waist and leaning against his side. "We were so lucky
to find this place. So secluded, yet only about half an
hour from Portland and the Jetport. I'll bet you can
fly to New York from here in almost the time it took
you to drive in from Connecticut. Do you know how
rarely anything comes up for sale on Prouts Neck?"

"Hmmm," he murmured, more interested in the
dynamics of her bikini top than in the view. "I should
know. That real-estate agent practically did hand-
springs over her commission."

"She should have. The commission on fifteen acres
of oceanfront land, including a protected cove with
private beach and a sixteen-room house, doesn't come
along every day. Of course, neither does a property
like this."

"Have you thought any more about what you'd like
to do with the rest of the land?" he asked, trying to
divert her attention from his exploring fingers.

"Let's leave it wild for now," she said, laughing
up at him as she caught his hand. "Behave yourself.
We're right out here in sight of our very proper housekeeper, the sea gulls, and any fisherman who passes
by. Come on, Lord Nimber Fingles. I'll find your
shirt before you forget where you're going."

"I know where I'd like to go."

"Later, you satyr."

"Is that any way to talk to the man who's about to
whisk you away for two romantic months in Aus-

tralia?" he asked plaintively as they crossed the veranda toward the open doors to the central hall.

"I'm not sure about the romantic part, but it will certainly be interesting. Have you told Arthur yet that you're bringing not only your wife and Gavin but also an eight-month-old baby and her nanny?"

"Oh, yes," answered Nick, grinning down at her as they mounted the stairs. "But don't ask me to repeat what he said. The only thing that got a favorable comment was the news that we were traveling in a private jet. You see how handy it is to be on borrowing terms with the super-rich?"

"It's not exactly the same as running next door for a cup of sugar! You must admit—"

"No, I don't," he said firmly. "After all, the Cattons have borrowed the family's yacht a couple of times on the same terms. So, for the cost of operating expenses we get to make a twenty-hour trip in comfort with real beds, decent-sized bathrooms, freshly cooked food—"

"A plush lounge, and room to cart along all Abby's gear," finished Cami. "Okay, I'll stop arguing. But you do have to admit there's something slightly decadent about flying around the world in a private jet."

"But, elf, only if it's just for pleasure. This is business. Have you really looked at that tour schedule? Believe me, you'll be glad to have the plane before we're through. Besides," he added with a sly look, "it's time you joined the mile-high club, and it's so much easier and more comfortable in a private plane."

Cami pushed him down on the window seat and started searching for a shirt. "You think I don't know what it is, but I do—especially when you mention it with that gleam in your eye." She gave him back a sly look of her own. "Oh, well, with all those long hours of night flying, and with Gavin and Nanny

Forbes to look after Abby, I suppose we'll have to find something interesting to do to pass the time, and—"

"Witch!"

Nick dived for her and tumbled her across the big bed. Her laughter as much as his superior strength defeated her, and she collapsed against his chest, gasping for breath. He looked up into her glowing face with suddenly serious eyes.

"To think I almost lost you through sheer stupidity. These past two years have been like a miracle. Are you as happy as I am, *cara?*"

"How can you ask, you twit? I've got you and Abby, this beautiful home—not that I wasn't happy in the place we rented in Falmouth Foreside, but this one's really ours—and I've got the ocean at my doorstep, a marvelous excuse to see the world occasionally, great people to keep everything running smoothly, and it's all an easy drive from the shop!"

"Cami—"

"Hey! I almost forgot. The sign for the front gate was delivered at noon. Gavin said he'd put it up when he gets back with Abby, and I called Jean and Ronan to come down for supper so we can have an official unveiling."

"I'm almost afraid to ask what name you picked." Nick eyed her gleeful expression suspiciously. "You couldn't possibly have had that atrocious pun cast in brass. Did you?"

"You'll just have to wait and see." She tried to look wistful as she asked, "It wasn't really that atrocious, was it? You have to admit it was appropriate."

"All right, I'll admit it, but still . . ."

"Don't fret about it now. You've got to get a move on or you'll be late for the ladies. Just wait until later. I promise you'll love it. The plaque is beautiful, and

I've got a bottle of champagne all ready for the christening ceremony."

"Speaking of ceremonies," he murmured, rolling over and pinning her beneath him, "aren't you going to kiss me good-bye?"

"But you're not ready to leave yet," she protested, laughing up at him.

"Don't you know," he whispered as he began nibbling kisses from her ear across her cheek, "that every ceremony . . . requires a rehearsal? So . . . practice now . . . perform later."

Cami's pithy retort faded away unnoticed as she concentrated on answering the demands of his warm, eager mouth.

"Is everybody ready?" asked Cami, bubbling with excitement.

The small group standing at the edge of the driveway, just off the street, chorused acknowledgment and lifted their full champagne glasses expectantly. Cami scanned the group one last time to be sure everyone was there. Mrs. Grayson, Nanny Forbes, and Gavin stood together a few feet from Jean, Ronan, and Nick, who was balancing a sleepy Abigail in one arm.

"I thought you were going to break the champagne over the sign," said Nick.

"Don't be silly. I bought this with my own money, and I'm not about to waste it. Okay, everyone, here goes!"

Cami lifted her glass in one hand, and with the other took hold of the sheet that was loosely draped over the three-foot-square, six-foot-high brick gatepost. "I hereby declare our new home officially christened . . ."

A hard yank and the sheet tumbled to the ground, revealing a large, gleaming brass plaque. Cami gestured dramatically to it, and turned to gauge her audience's reaction.

"What else could it be?" groaned Ronan, shaking his head in mock despair.

Gavin, Nanny Forbes, and the housekeeper, Mrs. Grayson, hesitantly smiled.

"You really did it," said Nick, laughing at his smug wife. "You realize, of course, that we'll never live this down."

Jean lifted her glass toward her best friend. "Only you, you total featherwit, would blow half a summer's income to cast a pun in brass."

"But it was so absolutely perfect, I couldn't resist!" Cami lilted, standing back to admire the elegantly simple nameplate.

Glowing in the evening sun, the polished brass plaque proudly proclaimed this to be the entrance to:

SEA AND SYMPHONY

WATCH FOR 6 NEW TITLES EVERY MONTH!

Second Chance at Love

All of the above titles are $1.75 per copy except where noted

All Titles are $1.95

DON'T MISS THESE TITLES
IN THE
SECOND CHANCE AT LOVE SERIES